THE

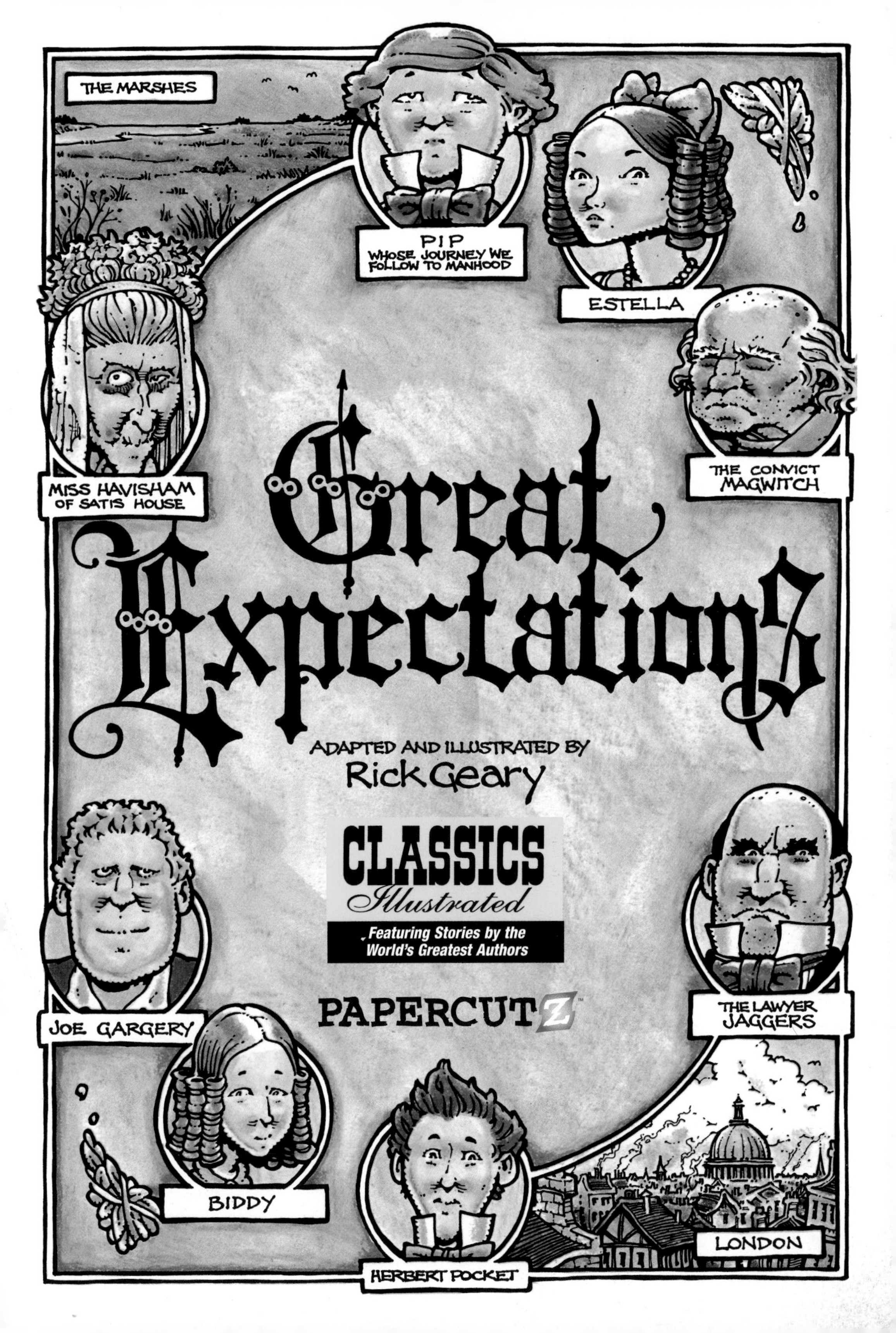
THE MARSHES
PIP
WHOSE JOURNEY WE FOLLOW TO MANHOOD
ESTELLA
MISS HAVISHAM
OF SATIS HOUSE
THE CONVICT
MAGWITCH
Great Expectations
ADAPTED AND ILLUSTRATED BY
Rick Geary
CLASSICS
Illustrated
Featuring Stories by the
World's Greatest Authors
PAPERCUTZ
JOE GARGERY
THE LAWYER
JAGGERS
BIDDY
HERBERT POCKET
LONDON

CLASSICS ILLUSTRATED GRAPHIC NOVELS AVAILABLE FROM PAPERCUTZ

CLASSICS ILLUSTRATED DELUXE:

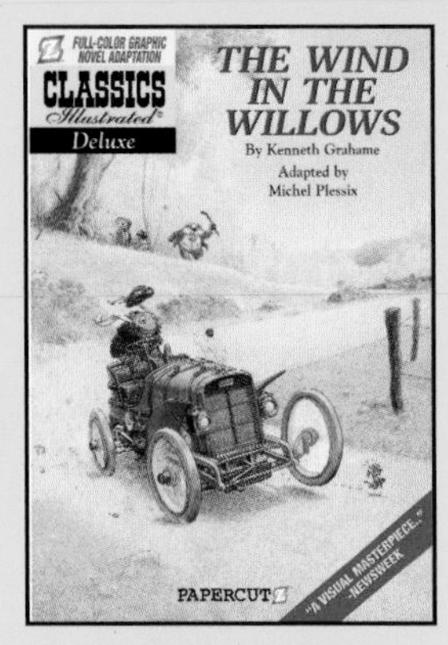

Graphic Novel #1 "The Wind In The Willows"

Graphic Novel #2 "Tales From The Brothers Grimm"

Graphic Novel #3 "Frankenstein"

CLASSICS ILLUSTRATED:

#1 "Great Expectations"

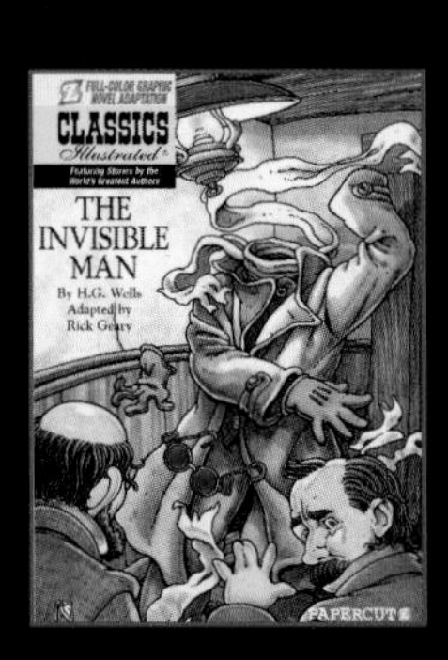

#2 "The Invisible Man"

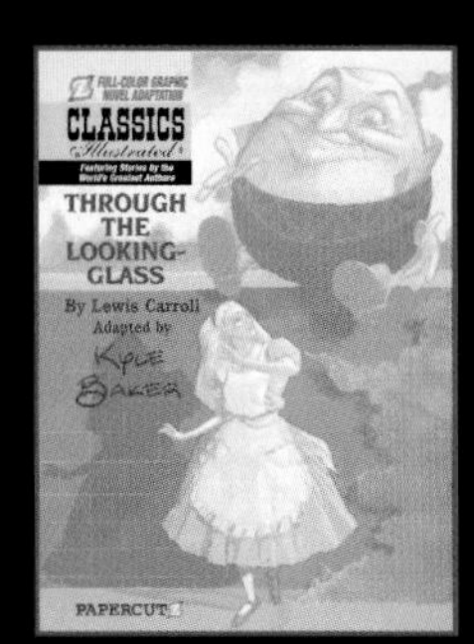

#3 "Through the Looking-Glass"

#4 "The Raven and Other Poems"

Classics Illustrated Deluxe are available for $13.95 each in paperback and $17.95 in hardcover. Classics Illustrated are available only in hardcover for $9.95 each. Please add $4.00 for postage and handling for the first book, add $1.00 for each additional book. MC, Visa, Amex excepted or make check payable to NBM Publishing.

Send to: **Papercutz, 40 Exchange Place, Suite 1308, New York, NY 10005 • 1-800-866-1223**

WWW.PAPERCUTZ.COM

Featuring Stories by the World's Greatest Authors

GREAT EXPECTATIONS

By Charles Dickens
Adapted by Rick Geary

PAPERCUTZ™
New York

Great Expectations
By Charles Dickens
Adapted by Rick Geary
Wade Roberts, Original Editorial Director
Alex Wald, Original Art Director
Jim Salicrup
Editor-in-Chief

ISBN 13: 978-1-59707-097-3
ISBN 10: 1-59707-097-1

Distributed by Macmillan.

10 9 8 7 6 5 4 3 2

Printed in China
February 2009 by Wing King Tong Co.
3/F Phase I Leader Industrial Centre
188 Texaco Road, Tseun Wan, N.T.
Hong Kong

MY FATHER'S FAMILY NAME BEING PIRRIP, AND MY CHRISTIAN NAME PHILLIP, MY INFANT TONGUE COULD MAKE OF BOTH NAMES NOTHING LONGER AND MORE EXPLICIT THAN PIP. SO I CALLED MYSELF PIP, AND CAME TO BE CALLED PIP.
AS I NEVER KNEW MY FATHER OR MY MOTHER, AND NEVER SAW ANY LIKENESS OF THEM, MY IDEAS REGARDING WHAT THEY WERE LIKE WERE LIKELY TO SPRING FROM MY OWN IMAGINATION AS I VISITED THEIR TOMBSTONES IN OUR VILLAGE CHURCHYARD.

OURS WAS THE MARSH COUNTRY, DOWN BY THE RIVER, WITHIN TWENTY MILES OF THE SEA. MY FIRST MOST VIVID AND BROAD IMPRESSION OF THE IDENTITY OF THINGS CAME ONE RAW AFTERNOON TOWARDS EVENING. IT WAS CHRISTMAS EVE, AND I WAS BUT SEVEN.

SOB

AT SUCH A TIME, I WAS PAINFULLY AWARE OF MY WORLD: THE BLEAK CHURCHYARD, THE DARK, FLAT WILDERNESS OF THE MARSHES, THE LEADEN RIVER, THE DISTANT, SAVAGE SEA, AND MOST ESPECIALLY OF MYSELF, A SMALL BUNDLE OF SHIVERS, STARTING TO CRY.

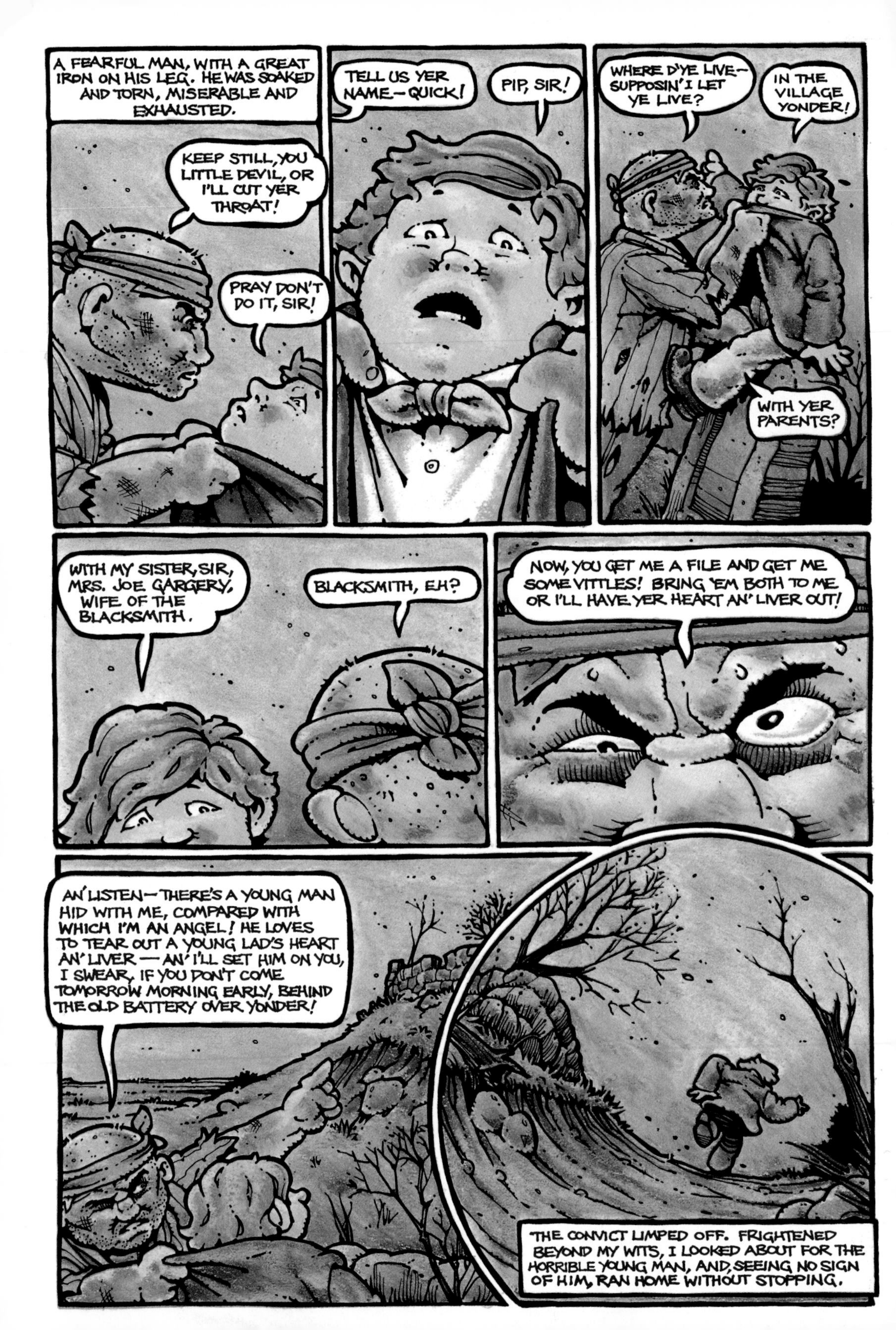
A FEARFUL MAN, WITH A GREAT IRON ON HIS LEG. HE WAS SOAKED AND TORN, MISERABLE AND EXHAUSTED.
KEEP STILL, YOU LITTLE DEVIL, OR I'LL CUT YER THROAT!
PRAY DON'T DO IT, SIR!
TELL US YER NAME—QUICK!
PIP, SIR!
WHERE D'YE LIVE—SUPPOSIN' I LET YE LIVE?
IN THE VILLAGE YONDER!
WITH YER PARENTS?
WITH MY SISTER, SIR, MRS. JOE GARGERY, WIFE OF THE BLACKSMITH.
BLACKSMITH, EH?
NOW, YOU GET ME A FILE AND GET ME SOME VITTLES! BRING 'EM BOTH TO ME OR I'LL HAVE YER HEART AN' LIVER OUT!
AN' LISTEN—THERE'S A YOUNG MAN HID WITH ME, COMPARED WITH WHICH I'M AN ANGEL! HE LOVES TO TEAR OUT A YOUNG LAD'S HEART AN' LIVER — AN' I'LL SET HIM ON YOU, I SWEAR, IF YOU DON'T COME TOMORROW MORNING EARLY, BEHIND THE OLD BATTERY OVER YONDER!
THE CONVICT LIMPED OFF. FRIGHTENED BEYOND MY WITS, I LOOKED ABOUT FOR THE HORRIBLE YOUNG MAN, AND, SEEING NO SIGN OF HIM, RAN HOME WITHOUT STOPPING.

HOME FOR ME WAS THE SMALL, RUDE SMITH'S COTTAGE ON THE VILLAGE EDGE.

MY SISTER, MRS. JOE GARGERY, WAS MORE THAN TWENTY YEARS OLDER THAN I, AND HAD ESTABLISHED A GREAT REPUTATION IN THE NEIGHBORHOOD BECAUSE SHE HAD BROUGHT ME UP "BY HAND."

WHERE HAVE YOU BEEN, YOU YOUNG MONKEY?

ONLY TO THE CHURCHYARD.

CHURCHYARD! IF IT WARN'T FOR ME, YOU'D HAVE BEEN THERE LONG AGO— AND STAYED THERE!

BUT JOE WAS MY FRIEND, A SWEET-TEMPERED, EASY-GOING, FOOLISH, DEAR FELLOW— A SORT OF HERCULES IN STRENGTH, AND ALSO IN WEAKNESS.

SIT HERE BY ME, PIP OLD CHAP. IT DON'T DO TO BE OUT TONIGHT— WE HEAR THERE'S CONVICTS ESCAPED ON THE MARSHES.

THE NEXT MORNING—CHRISTMAS DAY—I STOLE DOWNSTAIRS AS THE FIRST HINT OF LIGHT STREAKED THE SKY...

FROM THE PANTRY, I TOOK SOME BREAD, CHEESE, A BOTTLE OF BRANDY...

AND A BEAUTIFUL, ROUND, COMPACT PORK PIE.

FROM THE FORGE, ONE OF JOE'S FILES.

AND I RAN OUT ONTO THE MISTY MARSHES.

I SCRAMBLED UP A MOUND AND SUDDENLY SAW MY CONVICT.
STEALING UP SOFTLY, I TOUCHED HIM ON THE SHOULDER... BUT IT WAS NOT THE SAME MAN!
IT'S THE HORRIBLE YOUNG MAN, I THOUGHT, AS HE SWUNG WEAKLY AT ME...
THEN HE HOBBLED AWAY INTO THE MIST.
I WAS SOON AT THE BATTERY AND FOUND THE RIGHT MAN.
HE WAS GRATEFUL FOR THE FOOD AND ATE RAVENOUSLY.
I'M GLAD YOU ENJOY IT.
THANKEE, MY BOY, I DO.
I'M AFRAID THERE'S NO FOOD FOR THE YOUNG MAN YOU SPOKE OF. I CAME UPON HIM JUST NOW... I THOUGHT HE WAS YOU!
WHERE, BOY, WHERE?!
ON A HILL YONDER, BUT HE RAN OFF.
HE TOOK THE FILE, AND I LEFT HIM MUTTERING, AS HE SET TO WORK ON THE LEG-IRON
CURSE THE RAT... I'LL GET HIM... I'LL PULL HIM DOWN LIKE A BLOODHOUND!
THE LAST I HEARD OF HIM, I STOPPED IN THE MIST TO LISTEN, AND THE FILE WAS STILL GOING.

THAT DAY BEING CHRISTMAS, WE HAD GUESTS TO DINNER: MR WOPSLE, THE CLERK AT CHURCH; MR. HUBBLE, THE WHEELWRIGHT, AND MRS. HUBBLE; AND UNCLE PUMBLECHOOK (JOE'S UNCLE, MRS. JOE APPROPRIATED HIM), A WELL-TO-DO MERCHANT IN THE NEAREST TOWN.
I WAS SQUEEZED IN AT AN ODD ANGLE AND NOT ALLOWED TO SPEAK, AND GIVEN THE MOST OBSCURE SCRAPS TO EAT.
I SHOULD NOT HAVE MINDED IF ONLY THEY'D LEFT ME ALONE.
WHY IS IT THE YOUNG ARE NEVER GRATEFUL?
NATURALLY VICIOUS, THEY IS.
TRUE, TRUE.
ADDING TO THIS WAS MY SECRET SHAME AND GUILT... AND THE FEAR THAT AT ANY MOMENT MY CRIME WOULD BE FOUND OUT!
NOW WE MUST SAMPLE A DELIGHTFUL PRESENT FROM UNCLE PUMBLECHOOK — A SAVORY PORK PIE!
SHE WENT INTO THE PANTRY, AND I COULD BEAR IT NO MORE. I RAN FOR MY LIFE...
BUT GOT NO FURTHER THAN THE FRONT DOOR...
HERE YOU ARE, LOOK SHARP! COME ON!

I'M ON A CHASE IN THE NAME OF THE KING, AND I NEED THE BLACKSMITH!
JOE REPAIRED THE LEG-IRON, AND THEN HE ASKED THE SERGEANT IF WE MIGHT ACCOMPANY HIM AND HIS MEN OUT ONTO THE MARSHES.
WE HADN'T GONE FAR WHEN WE HEARD WILD SHOUTS AND CRIES.
IT WAS MY CONVICT AND THE OTHER MAN, LOCKED IN DEADLY COMBAT.
THEY WERE PRIED APART AND TAKEN INTO CUSTODY.
HE TRIED TO MURDER ME! BEAR WITNESS! I'D BE A DEAD MAN IF YOU'D NOT COME!
AT LAST MY CONVICT LOOKED ABOUT AND SAW ME . . .
AS WE WAITED BY THE RIVER FOR THE PRISON BOAT, HE MADE AN UNEXPECTED CONFESSION.
I TOOK SOME VITTLES LAST NIGHT, UP AT THE VILLAGE OVER YONDER—FROM THE BLACKSMITH'S.
I'M THE BLACKSMITH.
I'M SORRY TO SAY I TOOK SOME BRANDY AND A PORK PIE, AND ALSO A FILE . . .
WE DON'T KNOW WHAT YOU'VE DONE, BUT WE WOULDN'T HAVE YOU STARVED TO DEATH FOR IT. WOULD US, PIP?
THEN WE SAW THE MEN PUT INTO A BOAT, ROWED BY A CREW OF FELLOW PRISONERS, AND TAKEN TO THE BLACK HULK MOORED OFFSHORE.

IT WAS MUCH UPON MY MIND TO TELL JOE THE WHOLE TRUTH, YET I DID NOT, FOR I FELT HE WOULD THINK ME WORSE THAN I WAS.
WHEN THE TIME CAME, I WAS TO BE HIS APPRENTICE.
AND HE WAS MY REFUGE AGAINST THE RAMPAGES OF MRS. JOE.
WHO BROUGHT YOU UP BY HAND?
YOU DID.
AND WHY DID I DO IT?
I DON'T KNOW.
I DON'T KNOW EITHER, YOU UNGRATEFUL WRETCH! AND I'D NEVER DO IT AGAIN!
DON'T CRY, PIP— YOU AN' ME IS EVER THE BEST OF FREINDS.
ONE EVENING, ABOUT A YEAR AFTER THE EVENTS JUST RELATED, MRS. JOE AND UNCLE PUMBLECHOOK CAME HOME WITH NEWS DESTINED TO CHANGE MY LIFE FOREVER.
IF THE BOY AIN'T GRATEFUL TONIGHT, HE NEVER WILL BE!
OLD MISS HAVISHAM, IN THE BIG HOUSE UP TOWN— SHE ASKED UNCLE PUMBLECHOOK IF HE KNEW OF A BOY TO GO PLAY THERE!
SHE WANTS THIS BOY!
AND OF COURSE HE'S GOING, AND HE HAD BETTER PLAY THERE!

EVERYBODY FOR MILES ROUND HAD HEARD OF MISS HAVISHAM UP TOWN — AN IMMENSELY RICH AND GRIM LADY WHO LIVED IN A LARGE, DISMAL HOUSE CALLED SATIS — AND WHO LIVED A LIFE OF SECLUSION.
SATIS
SATIS

A YOUNG LADY CAME ACROSS THE COURTYARD WITH KEYS IN HER HAND.

WHAT'S YOUR NAME, BOY?
PIP.

SHE WAS ABOUT MY OWN AGE BUT SEEMED MUCH OLDER, BEING BEAUTIFUL AND SELF-POSSESSED.

PIP, IS IT? FOLLOW ME.

SHE LED ME ACROSS THE COURTYARD AND INTO THE HOUSE . . .

AND DOWN A LONG CORRIDOR. THERE WAS NOT A SINGLE LIGHT IN THE ENTIRE HOUSE.

AT LAST WE ENTERED WHAT LOOKED LIKE A DRESSING-ROOM, AND THERE, ARRAYED IN AN ANCIENT BRIDAL GOWN, SAT THE STRANGEST WOMAN I HAVE EVER SEEN, OR SHALL EVER SEE.
WHO IS IT?
PIP, MA'AM... MR. PUMBLECHOOK'S BOY, COME TO PLAY.
COME NEARER- LET ME LOOK AT YOU... COME CLOSE.
ARE YOU NOT AFRAID OF A WOMAN WHO HAS NEVER SEEN THE SUN SINCE YOU WERE BORN?
NO...
I LIED.
DO YOU KNOW WHAT I TOUCH HERE?
YOUR HEART?
BROKEN!
SO I AM TIRED AND NEED DIVERSION, AND I HAVE A SICK FANCY THAT I WANT TO SEE SOME PLAY. SO PLAY... PLAY, PLAY, PLAY!
BEG YOUR PARDON, MA'AM?
ARE YOU SULLEN AND OBSTINATE?
NO, MA'AM. I AM VERY SORRY FOR YOU, AND SORRY I CAN'T PLAY JUST NOW— BUT IT'S SO NEW HERE, AND SO STRANGE AND FINE AND MELANCHOLY.
SO NEW TO HIM, SO OLD TO ME... ESTELLA, LET ME SEE YOU PLAY CARDS WITH THIS BOY.
WITH THIS BOY? WHY HE'S A COMMON LABORING-BOY.
WELL? YOU CAN BREAK HIS HEART.
SO WE SAT DOWN TO CARDS— MISS HAVISHAM WATCHING, SILENTLY.

WHAT COARSE HANDS HE HAS, AND WHAT THICK BOOTS.
HER CONTEMPT FOR ME WAS SO STRONG IT BECAME INFECTIOUS, AND I CAUGHT IT.

AFTER OUR CARD GAME, ESTELLA LED ME TO THE COURTYARD, LEAVING ME THERE WITH SOME BREAD AND MEAT FOR MY LUNCH.
YOU ARE TO EAT HERE, BOY.

I HAD NEVER BEEN TROUBLED BY MY HANDS AND BOOTS BEFORE, BUT MY OPINION OF THOSE APPENDAGES WAS RAPIDLY DROPPING.

I WAS SO HUMILIATED, HURT, SPURNED, OFFENDED, ANGRY, THAT TEARS STARTED TO MY EYES...

AS I CRIED, I KICKED THE WALL AND TOOK A HARD TWIST TO MY HAIR, SO BITTER WERE MY FEELINGS.

AT LAST SHE RETURNED TO LET ME OUT THE GATE.
YOU HAVE BEEN CRYING, HAVEN'T YOU? AND YOU ARE NEAR CRYING AGAIN NOW.

DELIGHTED TO HAVE BEEN THE CAUSE OF MY TEARS, SHE GAVE A CONTEMPTUOUS LAUGH, PUSHED ME OUT, AND LOCKED THE GATE.

THIS WAS A MEMORABLE DAY, FOR IT MADE GREAT CHANGES IN ME. BUT IT IS THE SAME WITH ANY LIFE. PAUSE, YOU WHO READ THIS, AND THINK OF THE LONG CHAIN OF IRON OR GOLD, OF THORNS OR FLOWERS, THAT WOULD NEVER HAVE BOUND YOU, BUT FOR THE FORMATION OF THE FIRST LINK ON ONE MEMORABLE DAY.

IT OCCURRED TO ME THE BEST WAY TO START MAKING MYSELF UNCOMMON WAS TO BE EDUCATED IN PRACTICAL KNOWLEDGE. TO THIS END, I APPROACHED BIDDY— A VILLAGE GIRL AND AN ORPHAN LIKE MYSELF.

WE ENTERED INTO AN AGREEMENT WHEREBY SHE IMPARTED FIGURES TO ME FROM HER CATALOG OF PRICES, AND GAVE ME LETTERS TO COPY.

I RETURNED TO MISS HAVISHAM'S THE FOLLOWING WEEK.
IT'S THE COARSE LITTLE WRETCH AGAIN— YOU ARE TO COME THIS WAY.
SHE GUIDED ME TO A DIFFERENT PART OF THE HOUSE. ON THE STAIRS, WE PASSED AN IMPOSING GENTLEMAN.
WHOM HAVE WE HERE?
A NEIGABORHOOD BOY—MISS HAVISHAM SENT FOR HIM.
WELL, BEHAVE YOURSELF.
I HAD NO IDEA WHO HE WAS, NOR ANY FORESIGHT THAT HE WOULD PLAY AN IMPORTANT PART IN MY LIFE.
THIS TIME, I MET MISS HAVISHAM IN A HUGE AND AIRLESS DINING HALL, ITS TABLE LAID OUT FOR A GRAND FEAST.
THIS IS WHERE I WILL BE LAID WHEN I AM DEAD. THEY SHALL COME AND LOOK AT ME HERE.
MY ATTENTION WAS DRAWN BY THE GROTESQUE CENTREPIECE. ITS FUNGUS-COVERED FORM WAS QUITE INDISTINGUISHABLE.
I SAW SPECKLED-LEGGED SPIDERS AND BLACK BEETLES RUNNING HOME TO IT.
I HEARD MICE, TOO, RATTLING ABOUT BENEATH THE TABLE.
WHAT DO YOU THINK THIS IS?
I CAN'T GUESS, MA'AM.

IT'S A BRIDAL CAKE—MINE! NOW, COME—WALK ME, WALK ME!
ACCORDINGLY, I STARTED AT ONCE. SHE LEANED ON MY SHOULDER, AND WE BEGAN WALKING AROUND THE PERIMETER OF THE ROOM.
I SAW THAT THE CLOCKS IN THIS ROOM, AS IN HER DRESSING ROOM, WERE ALL STOPPED AT TWENTY MINUTES TO NINE.
THIS WAS MISS HAVISHAM'S BIRTHDAY, AND SHE WAS VISITED BY FOUR MEMBERS OF THE POCKET FAMILY—WHOM I TOOK TO BE HER POORER RELATIONS. THEY WERE SARAH POCKET, GEORGIANA POCKET, CAMILLA AND RAYMOND, AND THEY SOMEHOW CONVEYED TO ME THAT THEY WERE ALL TOADIES AND HUMBUGS. MISS HAVISHAM DESPISED THEM.
DEAR MISS HAVISHAM, HOW WELL YOU LOOK!
I DO NOT! I AM YELLOW SKIN AND BONE.
POOR DEAR SOUL—NOT TO BE EXPECTED TO LOOK WELL, POOR THING. THE IDEA!
LATER, ESTELLA AND I PLAYED AT CARDS AGAIN . . . ONLY THIS TIME, SHE DID NOT CONDESCEND TO SPEAK TO ME.
DO YOU FIND HER PRETTY, PIP?
AND AGAIN, I WAS DISMISSED INTO THE COURTYARD WITH MY LUNCH. I WANDERED INTO A NEGLECTED, OVERGROWN GARDEN.
ROUNDING A CORNER, I FOUND MYSELF EXCHANGING STARES WITH A PALE YOUNG GENTLEMAN.
HALLOA, WHO LET YOU IN?
MISS ESTELLA.

AND WHO GAVE YOU LEAVE TO PROWL ABOUT?
MISS ESTELLA . . .
COME AND FIGHT!

WHAT COULD I DO BUT FOLLOW HIM? I'VE OFTEN ASKED MYSELF THE QUSTION SINCE, BUT WHAT COULD I DO?
I OUGHT TO GIVE YOU A REASON FOR FIGHTING.

HERE IT IS!

HE DODGED BACKWARDS AND FORWARDS IN A FRIGHTENING MANNER, THEN CLOSED IN TO FINISH ME OFF.

I NEVER HAVE BEEN MORE SURPRISED THAN WHEN I LET OUT MY FIRST BLOW . . .

AND SAW HIM LYING ON HIS BACK WITH A BLOODY NOSE.

HE WAS ON HIS FEET DIRECTLY, AND I LET OUT MY SECOND BLOW.

HE WAS ON HIS BACK AGAIN, LOOKING UP AT ME OUT OF A BLACK EYE.

EVERY TIME I KNOCKED HIM DOWN, HE GOT UP AGAIN. HIS SPIRIT INSPIRED ME WITH GREAT RESPECT. FINALLY . . .
THAT MEANS YOU HAVE WON!

THOUGH I HAD NOT PROPOSED THE CONTEST, I FELT BUT A GLOOMY SATISFACTION IN MY VICTORY. WE PARTED POLITELY.
GOOD AFTERNOON.
THE SAME TO YOU, SIR.

WHEN I RETURNED TO THE COURTYARD, ESTELLA WAS WAITING. SHE SHOWED NO CURIOSITY ABOUT MY BLOODY FACE AND RUMPLED CLOTHES.
COME HERE . . . YOU MAY KISS ME IF YOU LIKE.

I FELT THE KISS WAS GIVEN TO THE COARSE, COMMON BOY AS A PIECE OF MONEY TOSSED TO A BEGGAR—AND THAT IT MEANT NOTHING.

FROM THEN ON, I RETURNED TO MISS HAVISHAM'S EVERY ALTERNATE DAY AT NOON TO WALK HER ABOUT THE DINING HALL. SOMETIMES SHE WOULD HAVE ME PUSH HER IN A GARDEN CHAIR. IN THIS WAY, EIGHT MONTHS WENT BY AND THE OLD WOMAN AND I BECAME QUITE USED TO ONE ANOTHER.

HER RELATIONS, WHEN VISITING, REGARDED ME WITH SUSPICION.

ESTELLA WAS ALWAYS THERE TO LET ME IN AND OUT, BUT SHE NEVER ALLOWED ME TO KISS HER AGAIN.

MISS HAVISHAM CLEARLY ENJOYED TAUNTING ME WITH ESTELLA'S BEAUTY...

DOES SHE NOT GROW PRETTIER, PIP?

AND WOULD SUDDENLY EMBRACE HER WITH LAVISH FONDNESS.

BREAK THEIR HEARTS, MY PRIDE AND HOPE, AND HAVE NO MERCY!

WHAT COULD I BECOME IN THESE SURROUNDINGS?

HOW COULD MY CHARACTER FAIL TO BE INFLUENCED BY THEM?

AT HOME, MY SISTER AND UNCLE PUMBLECHOOK WOULD INDULGE IN SUCH NONSENSICAL SPECULATIONS ABOUT WHAT MISS HAVISHAM WOULD DO FOR ME, THAT I WOULD WANT TO BURST INTO TEARS AND PUMMEL THEM ALL OVER.

WHEN I REACHED MY TWELFTH YEAR, I WAS BOUND OVER TO JOE AS HIS APPRENTICE.

I NOW HAD A STRONG CONVICTION THAT I SHOULD NEVER LIKE JOE'S TRADE. I HAD ONCE BUT NO MORE.

IT IS A MOST MISERABLE THING TO BE ASHAMED OF HOME.

IT WAS AGREED THAT I WOULD CONTINUE TO CALL UPON MISS HAVISHAM EVERY YEAR ON MY BIRTHDAY. ON THE FIRST SUCH VISIT, THERE WAS NO ESTELLA.

SHE IS ABROAD, EDUCATING FOR A LADY— FAR OUT OF REACH, PRETTIER THAN EVER, ADMIRED BY ALL WHO SEE HER.

SHE SAID THESE WORDS WITH A MALIGNANT GLEE.

DO YOU FEEL THAT YOU HAVE LOST HER?

IN THIS DESPAIRING STATE OF MIND, I RETURNED HOME TO A GRIM DISCOVERY...

WHILE JOE WAS OUT, OUR HOUSE HAD BEEN VIOLENTLY ENTERED — AND MY SISTER ATTACKED AND HURT, DESTINED NEVER TO BE ON THE RAMPAGE AGAIN.

BESIDE HER ON THE FLOOR WAS FOUND A CONVICT'S LEG-IRON.

SHE REMAINED GREATLY DAZED AND SENSELESS, BARELY ABLE TO MAKE HER WISHES KNOWN ON A SLATE.

SCARCELY A MONTH AFTER THE TRAGEDY, BIDDY CAME TO US, WITH ALL HER WORLDLY EFFECTS IN A SMALL SPECKLED BOX.

SHE TOOK OVER THE CARE OF MRS. JOE WITH A FIRM, PATIENT HAND, AND MANAGED THE HOUSEHOLD WITH A CLEVERNESS THAT MADE ME MARVEL.

BUT I WAS UNHAPPY AT THE FORGE. I DREADED THAT I WOULD ONE DAY LIFT MY EYES AND SEE ESTELLA, WATCHING ME AT MY GRIMIEST AND COMMONEST.

WHATEVER KNOWLEDGE I ACQUIRED FROM BIDDY, I TRIED TO IMPART TO JOE, THAT HE MIGHT BE LESS IGNORANT AND COMMON, AND LESS OPEN TO ESTELLA'S REPROACH.

BIDDY AND I WOULD OFTEN TAKE WALKS ALONG THE RIVER, AND CONFIDE IN ONE ANOTHER. BIDDY WAS NEVER INSULTING OR CAPRICIOUS. ALL THAT SHE SAID SEEMED RIGHT. ONE AFTERNOON, I OFFERED HER A CONFESSION.

BIDDY, I WANT TO BE A GENTLEMAN.

OH, I WOULDN'T, IF I WAS YOU. I DON'T THINK IT WOULD DO AT ALL.
BUT I'M NOT AT ALL HAPPY AS I AM! I AM DISGUSTED WITH MY CALLING AND WITH MY LIFE! AND I SHALL NEVER BE ANYTHING BUT MISERABLE!
THAT'S A PITY.
THERE'S A BEAUTIFUL YOUNG LADY AT MISS HAVISHAM'S. SHE'S MORE BEAUTIFUL THAN ANYBODY EVER WAS, AND I ADMIRE HER DREADFULLY. BUT SHE THINKS ME COARSE AND COMMON, AND I WANT TO BE A GENTLEMAN ON HER ACCOUNT.
DO YOU WANT TO BE A GENTLEMAN TO SPITE HER OR TO GAIN HER OVER?
I DON'T KNOW.
BECAUSE, IF IT IS TO SPITE HER, THAT MIGHT BE BETTER CARRIED OUT BY CARING NOTHING FOR HER WORDS. AND IF IT IS TO GAIN HER OVER, I SHOULD THINK SHE WAS NOT WORTH GAINING OVER.
QUITE TRUE. JUST THE SAME, I ADMIRE HER DREADFULLY.
OH, BIDDY, .. I WISH YOU COULD PUT ME RIGHT.
I WISH I COULD...
IF ONLY I COULD MAKE MYSELF FALL IN LOVE WITH YOU.
ANYWAY, I AM GLAD THAT YOU HAVE FELT YOU COULD GIVE ME YOUR CONFIDENCE.
BIDDY, I SHALL ALWAYS TELL YOU EVERYTHING!
...TILL YOU'RE A GENTLEMAN.
ONE MOMENTOUS EVENING, IN THE FOURTH YEAR OF MY APPRENTICESHIP TO JOE, HE AND I WERE SITTING BY THE FIRE AT THE "THREE JOLLY BARGEMEN."

A LARGE, DARK MAN ENTERED THE TAVERN. I RECOGNIZED HIM AS THE IMPOSING GENTLEMAN I HAD PASSED ON MISS HAVISHAM'S STAIRS SO MANY YEARS BEFORE.
I HAVE REASON TO BELIEVE THERE IS A BLACKSMITH AMONG YOU NAMED JOSEPH GARGERY.
THAT BE ME, SIR.

YOU HAVE AN APPRENTICE, COMMONLY KNOWN AS PIP— IS HE HERE?
I AM HERE.

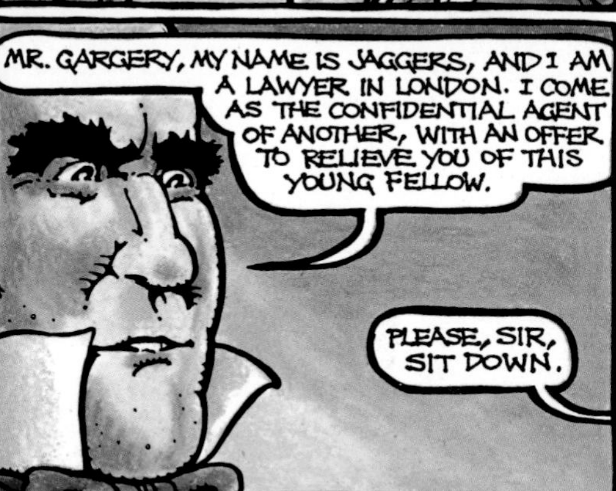
MR. GARGERY, MY NAME IS JAGGERS, AND I AM A LAWYER IN LONDON. I COME AS THE CONFIDENTIAL AGENT OF ANOTHER, WITH AN OFFER TO RELIEVE YOU OF THIS YOUNG FELLOW.
PLEASE, SIR, SIT DOWN.

I AM INSTRUCTED TO COMMUNICATE TO HIM THAT HE WILL COME INTO A HANDSOME PROPERTY.

IT IS THE DESIRE OF THE PRESENT HOLDER OF THAT PROPERTY THAT YOU BE REMOVED FROM THIS PRESENT SPHERE OF LIFE, AND FROM THIS PLACE, AND BE BROUGHT UP AS A GENTLEMAN . . .
IN A WORD, AS A YOUNG FELLOW OF GREAT EXPECTATIONS!

MY DREAM WAS OUT; MY WILD FANCY WAS SURPASSED BY SOBER REALITY. MISS HAVISHAM WAS GOING TO MAKE MY FORTUNE ON A GRAND SCALE!

YOU ARE TO UNDERSTAND, MR. PIP, THAT THE NAME OF YOUR LIBERAL BENEFACTOR IS TO REMAIN A PROFOUND SECRET, UNTIL THAT PERSON CHOOSES TO REVEAL IT.
YES, SIR.

YOU ARE MOST POSITIVELY PROHIBITED FROM MAKING ANY INQUIRY REGARDING THIS PERSON, AND IF YOU HAVE ANY SUSPICION IN YOUR BREAST, YOU ARE TO KEEP IT THERE.
YES, SIR.

THERE IS LODGED IN MY HANDS A SUM OF MONEY SUFFICIENT FOR YOUR EDUCATION AND MAINTENANCE IN LONDON. THERE IS A TUTOR I KNOW OF—A MR. MATTHEW POCKET—WHO MIGHT SUIT THE PURPOSE.

I RECOGNIZED THE NAME—MISS HAVISHAM'S RELATION!

MR. JAGGERS SAID HE WAS AUTHORIZED TO MAKE JOE MONETARY COMPENSATION FOR THE LOSS OF MY ASSISTANCE.

IF YOU THINK AS MONEY CAN MAKE COMPENSATION TO ME FOR THE LOSS OF THIS CHILD—WHAT COME TO THE FORGE—AND EVER THE BEST OF FRIENDS.

PIP'S A GENTLEMAN OF FORTUNE, AN' GOD BLESS HIM FOR IT!

AT HOME, JOE AND BIDDY CONGRATULATED ME, BUT THERE WAS A TOUCH OF SADNESS IN THEM THAT I RATHER RESENTED.

THIS SHOULD HAVE BEEN THE HAPPIEST DAY OF MY LIFE. BUT, AS I LAY IN MY MEAN LITTLE ROOM, I FELL INTO THE SAME CONFUSED STATE OF MIND BETWEEN IT AND THE BETTER ROOMS TO WHICH I WAS GOING, AS I HAD BEEN SO OFTEN LATELY BETWEEN THE FORGE AND MISS HAVISHAM'S, BIDDY AND ESTELLA.

SIX DAYS LATER, I VISITED MISS HAVISHAM TO SAY FAREWELL. SHE GAVE NO HINT THAT SHE WAS MY BENEFACTRESS.

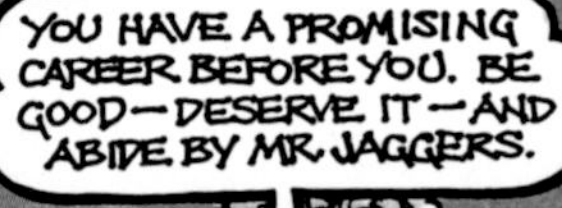

YOU HAVE A PROMISING CAREER BEFORE YOU. BE GOOD—DESERVE IT—AND ABIDE BY MR. JAGGERS.

THEN I FINALLY TOOK LEAVE OF BIDDY AND JOE. . .

AND I SET OFF FOR LONDON. THE MISTS HAD ALL SOLEMNLY RISEN NOW, AND THE WORLD LAY SPREAD BEFORE ME.

THUS ENDS THE FIRST STAGE OF PIP'S EXPECTATIONS

THE JOURNEY TO THE METROPOLIS WAS ONE OF ABOUT FIVE HOURS, AND I ARRIVED AT MIDDAY. WHILE I WAS SCARED BY THE IMMENSITY OF LONDON, I THINK I HAD SOME FAINT FEELINGS THAT IT WAS RATHER UGLY, CROOKED, NARROW AND DIRTY.
MY FIRST STOP WAS MR. JAGGERS' LEGAL ESTABLISHMENT.
YOUNG MR. PIP, COME IN. AS I HAVE BEEN APPOINTED YOUR GUARDIAN, YOU ARE TO COME TO ME FOR ANYTHING YOU NEED.
HE INTRODUCED ME TO HIS ASSOCIATE, THE DRY MR. WEMMICK.
AS I KEEP THE CASH, WE SHALL MOST LIKELY MEET OFTEN.
I WAS GIVEN DIRECTIONS TO "BARNARD'S INN," WHERE I WAS TO ROOM WITH A YOUNG MR. HERBERT POCKET.
BARNARD'S

WHEN WE MET, I RECOGNIZED HIM IMMEDIATELY.
MR. PIP?
MR. POCKET?
YOU'RE THE PROWLING BOY!
AND YOU'RE THE PALE YOUNG GENTLEMAN!
HE BADE ME WELCOME, AND I COULD SENSE THAT WE WOULD BE GREAT FRIENDS.
THE IDEA OF IT BEING YOU! PLEASE EXCUSE THE BARENESS. I HOPE YOU'LL BE ABLE TO MAKE OUT TOLERABLY WELL.
I SHALL HAVE NO TROUBLE AT ALL!
WE TALKED OF MISS HAVISHAM, AND OF HOW HE HAD VISITED SATIS HOUSE THAT DAY WITH HIS FATHER'S RELATIVES.
BOTH SHE AND ESTELLA REJECTED ME FOR A PLAYMATE. I GUESS YOU WERE THE FAVORED ONE.
MISS HAVISHAM HATES MY FATHER... DO YOU KNOW HER STORY?
NOT COMPLETELY. ONLY THAT SOMEBODY MUST HAVE DONE HER A GREAT INJURY YEARS AGO.
CORRECT! YOU SEE, TWENTY-FIVE YEARS AGO, MISS HAVISHAM WAS AN HEIRESS, AND MUCH SOUGHT AFTER FOR MARRIAGE. THERE APPEARED A CERTAIN GENTLEMAN WHO COURTED HER. BUT HER FAMILY, INCLUDING MY FATHER, KNEW HIM TO BE NO REAL GENTLEMAN. SHE WAS TOO MUCH IN LOVE TO HEAR COUNSEL: SHE ORDERED MY FATHER OUT OF HER HOUSE, AND THEY'VE NOT SEEN EACH OTHER SINCE...
WELL, THE MARRIAGE DAY WAS FIXED, ALL PLANS WERE SET. THE DAY CAME, BUT NOT THE BRIDEGROOM. HOWEVER, A LETTER ARRIVED...
AS SHE WAS DRESSING FOR THE WEDDING? AT TWENTY MINUTES TO NINE?
PRECISELY!
BUT HOW DID SHE COME TO RAISE ESTELLA? WHAT RELATION ARE THEY?
MISS HAVISHAM ADOPTED ESTELLA WHEN SHE WAS BUT AN INFANT... AND I'M AFRAID THAT'S ALL I KNOW.
POOR HERBERT WORKED IN A COUNTING-HOUSE, HE TOLD ME, WITH NO REAL PROSPECTS. I HAD THE IMPRESSION THAT HIS LIFE WOULD ALWAYS BE A STRUGGLE.

AFTER A FEW DAYS, HERBERT TOOK ME TO HIS FAMILY'S RESIDENCE AT HAMMERSMITH. HERE, HIS FATHER WOULD TUTOR ME.
IT WAS A JOLLY, CHAOTIC HOME, FILLED WITH TUMBLING CHILDREN!
MR. POCKET WAS A MAN IN A PERPETUAL STATE OF PERPLEXITY.
I AM GLAD TO SEE YOU, MR. PIP. I HOPE YOU ARE NOT SORRY TO SEE ME.
MR. JAGGERS TELLS ME YOU ARE NOT DESIGNED FOR ANY PROFESSION, BUT YOU ARE TO RECEIVE THE GENERAL EDUCATION SUITABLE TO ANY YOUNG MAN IN PROSPEROUS CIRCUMSTANCES.
I WAS INTRODUCED TO HIS TWO OTHER STUDENTS: DRUMMLE AND STARTOP.
BENTLEY DRUMMLE, NEXT HEIR BUT ONE TO A BARONETCY, MET WITH MY IMMEDIATE LOATHING...
OH, LORD...
HE WAS IDLE, PROUD, SUSPICIOUS, AND THICK-HEADED.
AND THUS I BEGAN MY EDUCATION, DIVIDING MY DAYS BETWEEN LONDON & HAMMERSMITH.
HERBERT WAS MY INTIMATE COMPANION, AND BETWEEN HIM AND HIS FATHER I GOT ON FAST. IN TIME, WE WERE ABLE TO FURNISH OUR ROOMS TO A COMFORTABLE FASHION.

AS A WELL-TURNED-OUT YOUNG GENTLEMAN, I SOON DEVELOPED EXPENSIVE HABITS, AND BEGAN TO SPEND AN AMOUNT OF MONEY THAT BEFORE I SHOULD HAVE THOUGHT FABULOUS.

I HIRED A YOUNG BOY OF THE NEIGHBORHOOD AS MY VALET, AND I CALLED HIM "THE AVENGER."

ALL THE WHILE, I CONTRACTED TREMENDOUS DEBTS, AS I EXHAUSTED MY MONTHLY ALLOWANCE.

I AM ALSO AFRAID I DREW HERBERT INTO MY EXTRAVAGANT LIFE, THOUGH I KNEW HE WAS FAR LESS ABLE TO STAND THE EXPENSE.

BUT HE FOLLOWED ALONG IN HIS AGREEABLE WAY, EVER CHEERFUL AND LOYAL.

ONE EVENING, I WENT WITH HERBERT AND DRUMMLE AND STARTOP TO DINNER AT MR. JAGGERS' HOME ON GERRARD STREET IN SOHO.

GENTLEMEN ... TO YOUR HEALTH AND SUCCESS!

I NOTICED HIS HOUSEKEEPER: SHE CREPT AROUND THE TABLE WITH A WILD AND HUNTED LOOK.

SUDDENLY, MR. JAGGERS GRABBED HER BY THE ARM.

SHOW THEM YOUR WRIST, MOLLY!

MASTER, DON'T!

THERE'S POWER HERE! VERY FEW MEN HAVE THE POWER OF WRIST THAT THIS WOMAN HAS!

MOLLY LOOKED AT EVERY ONE OF US IN REGULAR SUCCESSION, AS WE SAT AND WATCHED IN AWE.

AFTER SOME TIME HAD PASSED, I RECEIVED A LETTER FROM BIDDY TELLING ME OF JOE'S UPCOMING VISIT TO LONDON.

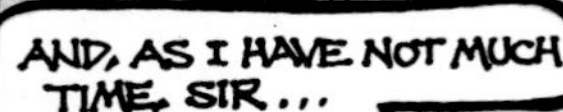

I WAS HAPPY THAT HE WOULD NOT VISIT HAMMERSMITH, WHERE HE MIGHT MEET DRUMMLE, WHOM I HELD IN CONTEMPT.

THUS, THROUGHOUT LIFE, WE COMMIT OUR WORST MEANNESSES FOR THE SAKE OF PEOPLE WHOM WE MOST DESPISE.

BY THAT TIME, HERBERT AND I HAD SECURED NEW AND GRANDER ROOMS AT GARDEN COURT, BESIDE THE RIVER.
I'M SO GLAD TO SEE YOU, JOE!
WHICH YOU HAVE GROWED, DEAR PIP, AND SWELLED AND GENTLE-FOLKED... AS TO BE SURE, YOU'RE A HONOR TO YOUR KING AND COUNTRY.

AND, AS I HAVE NOT MUCH TIME, SIR...
JOE! HOW CAN YOU CALL ME SIR?!

UM... AS I HAVE NOT MUCH TIME... UM... I WILL NOW TELL WHY I HAVE STOPPED HERE... MISS HAVISHAM, PIP, SHE WISHED TO SEE YOU... IF YOU COULD BE SO KIND AS TO COME DOWN TO SATIS HOUSE TOMORROW.

I ASKED JOE TO STAY TO DINNER, BUT HE WAS UNEASY IN MY PRESENCE. OUR OLD CLOSENESS WAS GONE.
PIP, I WISH YOU EVER WELL AND EVER PROSPERING TO A GREATER AND GREATER HEIGHT...
BUT YOU'RE NOT GOING NOW, JOE?!

YES, OLD CHAP, LIFE IS MADE OF EVER SO MANY PARTINGS WELDED TOGETHER... GOD BLESS YOU, DEAR PIP.

THE NEXT DAY, I TOOK LEAVE OF HERBERT AND BOARDED THE AFTERNOON COACH BACK TO OUR VILLAGE.
YOU'RE TO BE JOINED BY TWO CONVICTS BOUND FOR THE BOATYARDS.

ALL THE WAY DOWN, ONE OF THEM LOOKED ACROSS AT ME, APPRAISED MY WATCH AND CHAIN, AND OCCASIONALLY SPAT ON THE FLOOR.

WE PARTED AT THE CROSSROADS, THEY TO THE HULKS, I TO THE PLACE OF MY ORIGIN.

ON THE STREETS OF THE VILLAGE, I EXCITED MUCH ATTENTION WITH MY APPEARANCE.

LOOK, IT'S THE BLACKSMITH'S BOY!

I FOUND MISS HAVISHAM SEATED IN HER OLD CHAIR BY THE DRESSING TABLE. BESIDE HER SAT AN ELEGANT LADY WHOM I HAD NEVER SEEN.

THIS LADY LIFTED HER EYES TO ME, AND I SAW THAT THEY WERE ESTELLA'S EYES.

I FANCIED, AS I GREETED HER, THAT I HAD SLIPPED HOPELESSLY BACK INTO THE COARSE, COMMON BOY AGAIN.

H-HELLO... ESTELLA...

IS SHE MUCH CHANGED, PIP? IS SHE BEAUTIFUL, GRACEFUL? DO YOU ADMIRE HER?

THE UNQUALIFIED TRUTH WAS THAT I LOVED ESTELLA SIMPLY BECAUSE I FOUND HER IRRESISTIBLE.

WE WALKED IN THE RUINED GARDEN. SHE TOLD ME THAT SHE HAD JUST COME FROM FRANCE, AND THAT SHE WAS GOING TO LIVE IN LONDON.

YOUR CHANGE OF FORTUNE AND PROSPECTS HAS CHANGED YOUR CHOICE OF COMPANIONS, I WOULD THINK...
NATURALLY.

AND WHAT WAS FIT COMPANY FOR YOU ONCE WOULD BE QUITE UNFIT FOR YOU NOW?

AT THAT MOMENT, ANY LINGERING INTENTION OF MY GOING TO SEE JOE WAS PUT TO FLIGHT.

I LOOKED IN ESTELLA'S EYES—SOMETHING WAS BORNE IN UPON MY MIND . . . A RECOGNITION . . . WHAT WAS IT?

WHEN I COME UP TO LONDON, YOU ARE TO CALL ON ME, BUT YOU MUST KNOW THAT I HAVE NO HEART.
I KNOW BETTER. THERE COULD BE NO SUCH BEAUTY WITHOUT IT.

OH! I HAVE A HEART TO BE STABBED OR SHOT IN. BUT YOU KNOW WHAT I MEAN. I HAVE NO SOFTNESS THERE—NO SYMPATHY—NO SENTIMENT—THAT NONSENSE.

I'M SORRY, BUT I CANNOT BELIEVE WHAT YOU SAY.
YOU DON'T? VERY WELL. IT IS SAID, AT ANY RATE. . . MISS HAVISHAM WANTS US BACK BY NOW.

LATER, MISS HAVISHAM TOOK ME ASIDE WITH A RAVENOUS INTENSITY.
HOW DOES SHE USE YOU, PIP?

LOVE HER, LOVE HER! IF SHE FAVORS YOU, LOVE HER! IF SHE WOUNDS YOU, LOVE HER! I BRED HER AND EDUCATED HER TO BE LOVED! LOVE HER!

OBVIOUSLY, ESTELLA WAS INTENDED FOR ME, BUT WHEN WOULD SHE BEGIN TO SHOW INTEREST? WHEN SHOULD I AWAKEN THE HEART THAT WAS MUTE AND SLEEPING?

AH ME! I THOUGHT, WITH GRAND EMOTIONS, THAT THERE WAS NOTHING LOW IN LEAVING WITHOUT SEEING JOE. I KNEW SHE WOULD BE CONTEMPTUOUS OF HIM. JOE HAD BROUGHT TEARS TO MY EYES, BUT—GOD FORGIVE ME!—THEY HAD SOON DRIED.

WHEN, UPON MY RETURN, I CONFESSED TO HERBERT MY LOVE FOR ESTELLA, HE WAS NOT IN THE LEAST SURPRISED.
BUT I NEVER TOLD YOU...
TOLD ME! YOU NEVER TOLD ME WHEN YOU CUT YOUR HAIR, BUT I HAD THE SENSES TO PERCEIVE IT. YOU HAVE ALWAYS ADORED HER!
BUT I SAW HER YESTERDAY, HERBERT. AND IF I ADORED HER BEFORE, I NOW DOUBLY ADORE HER!
AND WHAT ARE HER VIEWS TOWARD YOU?
OH! SHE IS THOUSANDS OF MILES AWAY FROM ME...
MY DEAR HERBERT, I CANNOT TELL YOU HOW DEPENDENT AND UNCERTAIN I FEEL!
YOU CANNOT DETACH YOURSELF?
NO — IMPOSSIBLE!
BUT SHE IS INTENDED FOR YOU, IS SHE NOT? ALL WILL TURN OUT WELL!
WHAT A HOPEFUL DISPOSITION YOU HAVE!
I OUGHT TO, FOR I HAVE NOT MUCH ELSE.
SOON THEREAFTER, I RECEIVED A NOTE FROM ESTELLA: SHE WAS COMING TO LONDON BY THE NEXT DAY'S COACH — AND I WAS TO MEET HER!
RESTLESS AND EXCITED THE NEXT MORNING, I WALKED WITH MR. WEMMICK.
I AM GOING TO NEWGATE PRISON WITH SOME BUSINESS TO CONDUCT. PLEASE COME ALONG — IT MIGHT INTEREST YOU.
WHO BE TH' LAD, WEMMICK? YOUR NEW HELPER?
HE WAS A HIGHLY POPULAR FIGURE THERE, I COULD SEE, AS HE CARRIED ON HIS LEGAL CONSULTATIONS.
I REFLECTED HOW STRANGE IT WAS THAT MY LIFE SHOULD BE ENCOMPASSED BY THIS TAINT OF PRISON AND CRIME...
AND I HOPED THE STENCH WAS OFF MY PERSON BY THE TIME ESTELLA ARRIVED.
AGAIN, AS I LOOKED AT HER, I FELT THAT SAME FAMILIARITY. WHAT WAS IT?

I ESCORTED HER TO A HOUSE IN RICHMOND, WHERE SHE WAS TO LIVE.
I WILL LIVE, AT GREAT EXPENSE, WITH A LADY WHO HAS THE POWER TO TAKE ME ABOUT, INTRODUCE ME TO PEOPLE... IT IS ALL A PART OF MISS HAVISHAM'S PLAN FOR ME.
IN THE MONTHS TO COME, I HAUNTED RICHMOND. AND, WHEN NOT THERE, IT HAUNTED ME.
OH, PIP, WILL YOU NOT TAKE WARNING?
OF WHAT?
OF ME.
THIS IS NOT TO SAY SHE WAS NOT PAID COURT BY OTHER YOUNG GENTLEMEN, INCLUDING — MUCH TO MY DISQUIET — THE ODIOUS DRUMMLE.
MY POOR SISTER, NEVER HAVING REGAINED HER SENSES, FINALLY EXPIRED, AND I JOINED JOE AND BIDDY AT THE SERVICE. THEY KNEW BETTER THAN I THAT I WOULD LIKELY NEVER RETURN TO SEE THEM AGAIN.
ON THE DAY I TURNED TWENTY-ONE, I WAS TO COME INTO THE BULK OF MY PROPERTY. I WAS ASKED TO MR. JAGGERS' OFFICE.
I HAVE HERE A NOTE FOR FIVE HUNDRED POUNDS. FROM NOW ON, IT IS TO BE YOUR INCOME PER ANNUM.
IS MY BENEFACTOR TO BE MADE KNOWN TO ME TODAY?
NO, I'M AFRAID NOT, MR. PIP.
MR. WEMMICK, I WISH TO USE PART OF THIS MONEY TO SERVE A FRIEND — TO GET HIM A START IN COMMERCIAL LIFE.
I DON'T RECOMMEND IT, BUT NEVERTHELESS IT IS YOUR BUSINESS.
IN DUE COURSE, MR. WEMMICK FOUND A WORTHY YOUNG MERCHANT — A MR. CLARRIKER — WHO WANTED INTELLIGENT HELP AND WHO WANTED CAPITAL. HE TOOK HERBERT ON!
CLARRIKER & Co
IMPORTER
THE WHOLE BUSINESS WAS SO CLEVERLY MANAGED, HE HAD NOT THE LEAST SUSPICION OF MY HAND BEING IN IT.
DEAR FRIEND, YOU WON'T BELIEVE THE NEWS I HAVE!
I AM ON MY WAY, BY SOME STRANGE FORTUNE. NOW I SHALL BE ABLE TO MARRY MY BELOVED CLARA!
HOW WONDERFUL!
MY OWN LIFE FARED LESS WELL. I ESCORTED ESTELLA DOWN ONE SUNDAY TO VISIT MISS HAVISHAM.
HOW DOES SHE USE YOU, PIP, HOW DOES SHE USE YOU?

SHE WAS EVEN MORE FIERCELY ATTACHED TO ESTELLA THAN BEFORE.
YOU DRIFT AWAY— ARE YOU TIRED OF ME?
ONLY A LITTLE TIRED OF MYSELF.

SPEAK THE TRUTH, YOU INGRATE! YOU TIRE OF ME! OH, YOU STOCK AND STONE, YOU COLD, COLD HEART!

WHAT? YOU REPROACH ME FOR BEING COLD? AM I NOT WHAT YOU HAVE MADE ME? TAKE ALL THE PRAISE, TAKE ALL THE BLAME, BUT TAKE ME AS I HAVE BEEN MADE.
SO PROUD, SO HARD...

WHO TAUGHT ME?
BUT TO BE PROUD AND HARD TO ME, ESTELLA! TO BE PROUD AND HARD TO ME!

MOTHER BY ADOPTION— I OWE EVERYTHING TO YOU. BUT, IF YOU ASK ME TO GIVE YOU WHAT YOU NEVER GAVE ME, MY DUTY AND GRATITUDE CANNOT DO THE IMPOSSIBLE.

THAT NIGHT, SLEEP WOULD NOT COME UPON ME IN MY GUEST ROOM, AND I WANDERED THE HALLS OF SATIS. I SAW MISS HAVISHAM, MOVING AS A GHOST THROUGH THE HOUSE, MAKING A LOW, MISERABLE CRY AS SHE WENT.

MY TWENTY-THIRD BIRTHDAY CAME AND PASSED, AND NOT ANOTHER WORD HAD I HEARD AS TO MY EXPECTATIONS. I COULD SETTLE ON NO COURSE IN LIFE. I FELT RESTLESS AND INCOMPLETE.

HULLOA, UP THERE!

THEN, ONE COLD, RAINY NIGHT, MY WORLD CAME CRASHING IN UPON ME. THE CLOCK OF ST. PAUL'S HAD JUST STRUCK ELEVEN, HERBERT WAS AWAY, AND I WAS SITTING UP READING, WHEN I HEARD FOOTSTEPS ON THE STAIRS OUTSIDE.

A STRANGE-LOOKING OLD MAN WAITED ON THE LANDING.
I'M LOOKIN' FOR MR. PIP.
YES... THAT IS MY NAME. COME UP.
HE WAS CREASED AND WEATHER-HARDENED, BUT I KNEW HIM AT ONCE — IT WAS MY CONVICT!
SO YOU'RE PIP?
NOBLE PIP! YOU ACTED NOBLY TO ME, MY BOY, AND I HAVE NEVER FORGOT IT!
HIS MANNER REPULSED ME, AND I BACKED AWAY.
STAY AWAY! IF YOU ARE GRATEFUL FOR WHAT I DID AS A CHILD, I HOPE YOU HAVE SHOWN YOUR GRATITUDE BY MENDING YOUR WAYS...
BUT SURELY YOU MUST UNDERSTAND THAT I CANNOT WISH TO RENEW THAT CHANCE ACQUAINTANCE WITH YOU OF SO LONG AGO, UNDER THESE DIFFERENT CIRCUMSTANCES!
HE WAS WET AND WEARY. AGAIN, I TOOK PITY.
PLEASE SIT AND REST YOURSELF. WILL YOU DRINK SOMETHING BEFORE YOU GO?
WHEN I BROUGHT HIM A GLASS, I SAW THAT HIS EYES WERE FILLED WITH TEARS.
I APOLOGIZE FOR SPEAKING HARSHLY... I APPRECIATE YOUR COMING TO THANK ME, AND I WISH YOU WELL AND HAPPY.
I ASKED HIM HOW HE HAD BEEN LIVING THESE YEARS...
I'VE BEEN A SHEEP-FARMER AND STOCK-BREEDER, IN THE NEW WORLD, AND I'VE DONE WONDERFUL WELL... AND YOU TOO, PIP, LOOK AS IF YOU'VE DONE WELL SINCE YOU AND ME WAS OUT ON THEM SHIVERIN' MARSHES.
YES — I HAVE BEEN EDUCATED FOR A GENTLEMAN, AND I HAVE BEEN CHOSEN TO COME INTO PROPERTY.
I KNOW IT, DEAR BOY, I KNOW IT!

IT'S ME WHAT HAS DONE IT! YES, PIP, I'VE MADE A GENTLEMAN OF YOU!
WHAT?!

I SWORE THAT TIME, SURE AS I EVER EARNED A GUINEA, THAT GUINEA SHOULD GO TO YOU! SURE AS I EVER SPECULATED AND GOT RICH, YOU SHOULD GET RICH! I LIVED ROUGH, THAT YOU SHOULD LIVE SMOOTH! I WORKED HARD, THAT YOU SHOULD BE ABOVE WORK! YOU SEE, MY BOY, YOU SEE!?

THE ABHORRENCE IN WHICH I HELD THE MAN, THE DREAD WITH WHICH I SHRANK FROM HIM, COULD NOT HAVE BEEN EXCEEDED IF HE HAD BEEN SOME TERRIBLE BEAST!

IT WAS ME, SINGLE-HANDED! NEVER A SOUL KNEW BUT JAGGERS AND MYSELF. DIDN'T YOU EVER THINK IT MIGHT BE ME?
NO, NEVER, NEVER!

I'M YOUR SECOND FATHER, LAD! AND HOW GOOD-LOOKING YOU HAVE GROWED! THERE MUST BE BRIGHT EYES SOMEWHERE, EH? A YOUNG LADY YOU'VE YOUR HEART SET ON? SHE SHALL BE YOURS, IF MONEY CAN BUY HER!
OH, ESTELLA, ESTELLA!

MISS HAVISHAM'S INTENTIONS FOR ME WERE A MERE DREAM. ESTELLA WAS NOT DESIGNED FOR ME. I ONLY SUFFERED AT SATIS HOUSE AS A CONVENIENCE, A MODEL TO PRACTICE ON.

BUT THE SHARPEST PAIN OF ALL WAS THAT—FOR THIS CONVICT, GUILTY OF I KNEW NOT WHAT CRIMES—I HAD DESERTED JOE.

I PUT THE MAN TO BED IN HERBERT'S ROOM, AND SAT UP CONTEMPLATING THE WRETCHEDNESS OF MY POSITION.

THE CANDLES FLICKERED OUT, THE FIRE SLOWLY DIED, AND THE WIND AND RAIN ONLY INTENSIFIED THE THICK, BLACK DARKNESS.

THUS ENDS THE SECOND STAGE OF PIP'S EXPECTATIONS

THE NEXT MORNING, I TOOK STOCK OF MY VISITOR'S SITUATION.

MY NAME IS MAGWITCH, BOY, ABEL MAGWITCH. BUT WHERE I LIVE, THEY KNOW ME AS "PROVIS."

IT WEREN'T EASY FOR ME TO LEAVE THEM PARTS, AND IT WEREN'T SAFE. BUT I WAS DETERMINED TO SEE MY LAD. YOU SEE, I WAS SENT FOR LIFE, PIP. IT'S DEATH FOR ME TO COME BACK HERE.

NOTHING WAS NEEDED BUT THIS! THE WRETCHED MAN HAD RISKED HIS LIFE TO COME TO ME — AND I HELD IT THERE IN MY KEEPING.

I FELT I COULD DO NO BETTER THAN TO SECURE HIM QUIET LODGING NEARBY. FOR THE TIME BEING, HE WOULD BE MY UNCLE PROVIS, ON A VISIT FROM THE COUNTRY.

ESSEX

HOTEL

THAT MORNING, I CALLED UPON MR. JAGGERS.

DON'T TELL ME ANYTHING, MR. PIP. I AM NOT CURIOUS.

I WILL ONLY SAY THIS: I HAVE BEEN INFORMED BY A PERSON NAMED ABEL MAGWITCH THAT HE IS THE BENEFACTOR SO LONG UNKNOWN TO ME.

THAT IS THE MAN—IN NEW SOUTH WALES...

AND ONLY HE?

AND ONLY HE.

YOU'LL EXCUSE ME, SIR, I DO NOT THINK YOU AT ALL RESPONSIBLE, BUT I HAD ALWAYS SUPPOSED IT WAS MISS HAVISHAM.

AS YOU SAY—I AM NOT AT ALL RESPONSIBLE FOR THAT.

YET IT LOOKED SO LIKE IT, SIR...

NOT A PARTICLE OF EVIDENCE! TAKE NOTHING ON ITS LOOKS— TAKE EVERYTHING ON EVIDENCE!

I CANNOT BEGIN TO SAY WHAT A MYSTERY MY BENEFACTOR WAS TO ME. I TRIED TO CHANGE HIS APPEARANCE SOMEWHAT, BUT NOTHING COULD TAME HIS RUDE, SAVAGE AIR.

THANKEE, DEAR BOY.

THERE WAS NO GETTING AROUND IT: I COULD NEVER ACCEPT ANOTHER PENNY FROM HIM. I HAD TO GET HIM OUT OF ENGLAND, AND, TO DO THAT, I KNEW THAT I WOULD HAVE TO GO ABROAD WITH HIM.

WHEN HERBERT RETURNED, WE LET HIM IN ON OUR SECRET. PROVIS MADE HIM SWEAR ON A GREASY BIBLE THAT HE ALWAYS CARRIED WITH HIM.

KISS IT, LAD!

THAT EVENING, HERBERT AND I LISTENED RAPTLY AS THE OLD MAN TOLD US HIS STORY.
I WAS RAISED TO BE NOTHIN' BUT A VARMINT, LADS.

I FIRST BECAME AWARE OF MYSELF DOWN IN ESSEX, THIEVIN' TURNIPS FOR A LIVIN'. AND THAT WAS MY LIFE: TRAMPIN', BEGGIN', THIEVIN', WORKIN' SOMETIMES WHEN I COULD.

IT HAPPENED THAT I FELL IN WITH A MAN NAMED COMPEYSON. HE WAS SET UP FOR A GENTLEMAN, HE WAS: HE HAD LEARNING, AND HE WAS A SMOOTH TALKER, AND KNEW THE WAYS OF GENTLEFOLKS.

COMPEYSON TOOK ME ON AS PARTNER—THAT WAS OVER TWENTY YEARS AGO, NOW—AND WE HAD A CAREER OF SWINDLIN', FORGIN', AND SUCH-LIKE... UNTIL WE WAS CAUGHT.

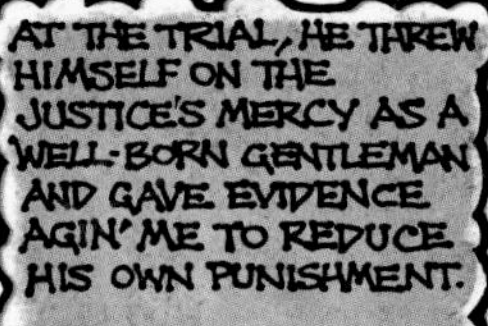
AT THE TRIAL, HE THREW HIMSELF ON THE JUSTICE'S MERCY AS A WELL-BORN GENTLEMAN AND GAVE EVIDENCE AGIN' ME TO REDUCE HIS OWN PUNISHMENT.

WELL, WE WAS BOTH SENT TO THE HULKS, AND I SWORE I'D CRACK HIS SKULL LIKE THE CLAW OF A LOBSTER, IF I EVER GOT MY CHANCE.

AS IT TURNED OUT, I TOOK MY CHANCE TO ESCAPE ONE NIGHT, AND IT WAS THERE ON THE MARSHES WHEN I FIRST SEEN MY DEAR BOY!

BY MY BOY, I WAS GIVEN TO UNDERSTAND THAT COMPEYSON WAS OUT ON THEM MARSHES TOO. I HUNTED HIM DOWN! I SMASHED HIS FACE! WOULD'VE KILLED HIM, TOO, IF WE WEREN'T FOUND. THEN I NEVER HEARD NO MORE OF HIM.

THE WORLD TOOK ITS PUNISHMENT ON ME, BUT ALL THE WHILE I FELT HAPPY, 'CAUSE IN SECRET I WAS MAKIN' A GENTLEMAN! THIS IS HOW I KEPT GOIN', DEAR PIP! PEOPLE MIGHT KICK DUST ON THIS OLD VARMINT, BUT—BLAST 'EM ALL!—I'LL SHOW 'EM A BETTER GENTLEMAN THAN THE LOT PUT TOGETHER!

WHEN PROVIS TURNED TO THE FIRE, HERBERT PASSED ME A NOTE...
COMPEYSON WAS THE NAME OF THE MAN WHO PROFESSED TO BE MISS HAVISHAM'S LOVER.

I FELT THAT, BEFORE GOING ABROAD, I MUST SEE BOTH MISS HAVISHAM AND ESTELLA. UPON LEARNING THAT ESTELLA WAS VISITING SATIS HOUSE, I WENT DOWN IMMEDIATELY.

AS I ARRIVED AT THE GATE, I FOUND, TO MY GREAT DISTRESS, BENTLEY DRUMMLE JUST LEAVING. WE SPOKE NOT A WORD.

INSIDE, MISS HAVISHAM AND ESTELLA SAT QUIETLY BY THE FIRE
AND WHAT WIND BLOWS YOU HERE, PIP?

MISS HAVISHAM, I JUST WANT YOU TO KNOW I AM ABOUT AS UNHAPPY AS YOU CAN EVER HAVE MEANT ME TO BE.

I HAVE FOUND OUT WHO MY PATRON IS — IT IS AN UNFORTUNATE DISCOVERY, NOT LIKELY TO ENRICH MY REPUTATION OR POSITION.

I FEEL, WHEN I FELL INTO THE MISTAKE I SO LONG REMAINED IN, YOU LED ME ON.
YES, I LET YOU BELIEVE CERTAIN THINGS . . .
WAS THAT KIND?

WHO AM I, FOR GOD'S SAKE, THAT I SHOULD BE KIND?!

IN HUMORING MY MISTAKE, YOU PUNISHED AND TORMENTED YOUR SELF-SEEKING RELATIONS.
I DID! THEY WOULD HAVE HAD IT SO! SO WOULD YOU! YOU MADE YOUR OWN SNARES, NOT I.

ESTELLA — LIKEWISE, MY LONG MISTAKE FORCED ME TO HOPE THAT MISS HAVISHAM MEANT US FOR ONE ANOTHER.

YOU KNOW I HAVE LOVED YOU LONG AND DEARLY. I HAVE NO HOPE THAT I SHALL EVER CALL YOU MINE — IN FACT, I AM IGNORANT OF WHAT MAY BECOME OF ME VERY SOON. STILL, I LOVE YOU, AND HAVE SINCE I FIRST SAW YOU IN THIS HOUSE.

WHEN YOU SAY YOU LOVE ME, I KNOW WHAT THE WORDS MEAN, BUT YOU TOUCH NOTHING HERE. I HAVE WARNED YOU OF THIS, HAVE I NOT?

I HOPED YOU COULD NOT MEAN IT. SURELY IT IS NOT IN NATURE.
IT IS IN MY NATURE . . . AND I MAKE A GREAT DIFFERENCE BETWEEN YOU AND ALL OTHERS BY TELLING YOU THAT, BELIEVE ME.

IS IT TRUE THAT BENTLEY DRUMMLE IS IN TOWN AND PURSUING YOU?
IT IS QUITE TRUE.

WHY DO YOU ENCOURAGE HIM? YOU CANNOT LOVE HIM, ESTELLA?! YOU WOULD NEVER MARRY HIM?!

WHY NOT TELL YOU THE TRUTH? I AM TO BE MARRIED TO HIM.

DEAREST ESTELLA— PUT ME ASIDE FOREVER BUT BESTOW YOURSELF ON A WORTHIER PERSON THAN DRUMMLE. HE'S A BRUTE — A MEAN AND STUPID BRUTE!

OH, DON'T BE AFRAID OF MY BEING A BLESSING TO HIM . . . COME NOW, MUST WE PART ON THIS NOTE? THIS WILL PASS — YOU WILL HAVE ME OUT OF YOUR THOUGHTS IN A WEEK.

OUT OF MY THOUGHTS?! YOU ARE PART OF MY EXISTENCE, PART OF MY SELF! YOU HAVE BEEN BEHIND MY EVERY THOUGHT SINCE I FIRST CAME HERE, AND YOU HAVE BEEN IN EVERY PROSPECT I HAVE SEEN — ON THE RIVER, ON THE MARSHES, IN THE STREETS, IN THE CLOUDS . . . YOU HAVE BEEN THE EMBODIMENT OF EVERY GRACEFUL FANCY MY MIND HAS KNOWN. TO THE LAST OF MY LIFE, ESTELLA, YOU WILL BE PART OF THE LITTLE GOOD IN ME, PART OF THE EVIL.
BUT, IN THIS PARTING, I ASSOCIATE YOU ONLY WITH THE GOOD, FOR YOU MUST HAVE DONE ME MORE GOOD THAN HARM.
GOD BLESS YOU . . . GOD FORGIVE YOU.

WHAT AN ECSTASY OF UNHAPPINESS! AS I TURNED TO LEAVE, I SAW IN MISS HAVISHAM'S FACE A GHASTLY STARE OF PITY AND REMORSE.

ALL DONE, ALL GONE! I COULD NOT BEAR TO SIT IN A COACH AND BE TALKED TO, SO I SET OFF TO WALK ALL THE WAY TO LONDON.

ARRIVING HOME AT DUSK, TIRED AND MUDDY, I ENTERED THE COURT THROUGH THE REAR GATE, WHERE I FOUND A NOTE — IN MR. WEMMICK'S HAND — AWAITING ME.
Don't go Home
I FLED TO A CHEAP ROOM IN COVENT GARDEN, AND SPENT A SLEEPLESS NIGHT WONDERING WHAT CATASTROPHE MAY HAVE BEEN AFOOT.
"DON'T GO HOME..." "DON'T GO HOME..."
IN THE MORNING, I CALLED UPON MR. WEMMICK AT HIS HOME IN WALWORTH.
COME IN, MR. PIP. I TRUST YOU RECEIVED MY MESSAGE.
WHILE SEEING TO BUSINESS AT NEWGATE YESTERDAY, I HEARD FROM A RELIABLE SOURCE THAT YOUR ROOMS ARE BEING WATCHED.
BY WHOM?
I SHOULDN'T HAZARD TO SAY, BUT HAVE YOU HEARD OF A MAN OF BAD CHARACTER NAMED COMPEYSON?
YES, I HAVE.
WELL... MY WORD HAS IT THAT HE HAS BEEN SEEN IN LONDON.
NOT BEING ABLE TO FIND ME, MR. WEMMICK EXPLAINED, HE HAD APPROACHED HERBERT, AND, TOGETHER, THEY HAD MOVED POOR PROVIS TO NEW QUARTERS: THE HOME OF HERBERT'S FIANCÉE, CLARA, AND HER AGED FATHER.
I THANKED MR. WEMMICK FOR HIS HELP, AND, TOGETHER, WE FORMED A PLAN TO SMUGGLE MY BENEFACTOR OUT OF THE COUNTRY AT A MOMENT'S NOTICE.
ON MY WAY HOME, I FANCIED THAT I WAS FOLLOWED.

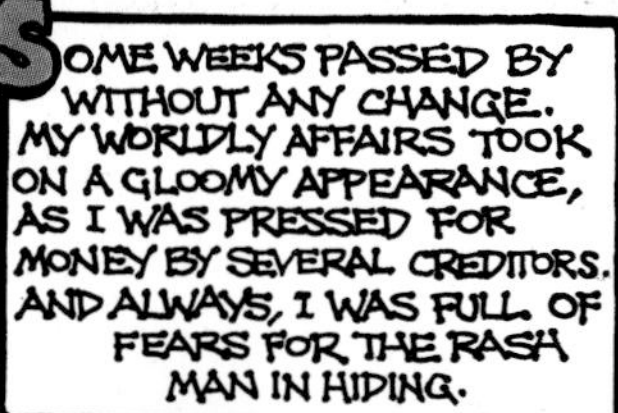

SOME WEEKS PASSED BY WITHOUT ANY CHANGE. MY WORLDLY AFFAIRS TOOK ON A GLOOMY APPEARANCE, AS I WAS PRESSED FOR MONEY BY SEVERAL CREDITORS. AND ALWAYS, I WAS FULL OF FEARS FOR THE RASH MAN IN HIDING.

THEN, ONE NIGHT, I WAS INVITED TO DINE, ALONG WITH MR. WEMMICK, AT MR. JAGGERS' HOME.
PIP, MISS HAVISHAM TELLS ME SHE WISHES TO SEE YOU ON A MATTER OF BUSINESS. YOU'LL GO DOWN?
OF COURSE.

MY ATTENTION TURNED AGAIN TO THE HOUSEKEEPER.
MOLLY, MOLLY... HOW SLOW YOU ARE THIS EVENING.

FORGIVE ME, MASTER

THIS TIME, MY GAZE WAS ARRESTED BY A CERTAIN MOVEMENT OF HER EYES AND TURN OF HER HEAD AS SHE SPOKE...

AND I FELT CERTAIN THAT THIS WOMAN WAS ESTELLA'S MOTHER!

AFTER WEMMICK AND I TOOK OUR LEAVE, I ASKED HIM ABOUT MOLLY.
SHE SEEMS LIKE A WILD BEAST.
YES, BUT JAGGERS HAS TAMED HER.

A SCORE OR SO YEARS AGO, SHE WAS TRIED FOR MURDER AT THE OLD BAILEY. SHE HAD BEEN KEEPING COMPANY WITH A MAN, AND, IN A RAGE OF JEALOUSY, SHE HAD FOUGHT ANOTHER WOMAN WHO WAS LARGER AND STRONGER THAN HERSELF. LATER, THAT WOMAN WAS FOUND BEATEN AND STRANGLED. BUT JAGGERS DEFENDED MOLLY, AND SHE WAS ACQUITTED.

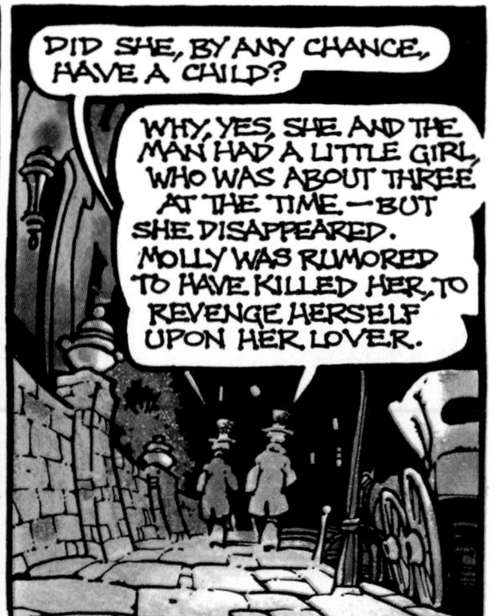

DID SHE, BY ANY CHANCE, HAVE A CHILD?
WHY, YES, SHE AND THE MAN HAD A LITTLE GIRL, WHO WAS ABOUT THREE AT THE TIME.—BUT SHE DISAPPEARED. MOLLY WAS RUMORED TO HAVE KILLED HER, TO REVENGE HERSELF UPON HER LOVER.

NOW, I WAS ABSOLUTELY CERTAIN.

ONCE AGAIN, I FOUND MISS HAVISHAM BY THE FIRE...
PIP, I WISH TO BE OF SERVICE TO YOU, TO MAKE AMENDS FOR WHAT I'VE DONE. BUT PERHAPS YOU CAN NEVER BELIEVE THAT THERE IS ANYTHING HUMAN IN MY HEART...
YOU CAN DO NOTHING FOR ME... BUT I WANT YOU TO KNOW YOU DEEPLY WRONG MR. MATTHEW POCKET AND HIS SON HERBERT, IF YOU BELIEVE THEM TO BE OTHERWISE THAN GENEROUS, LOYAL AND UPRIGHT.
AND IF YOU COULD SPARE THE MONEY TO DO MY FRIEND HERBERT A LASTING SERVICE, BUT ONE WHICH MUST BE DONE WITHOUT HIS KNOWLEDGE— I COULD SHOW YOU HOW... AND I WOULD BE VERY GRATEFUL. HE WILL NEED A RATHER LARGE SUM: NINE HUNDRED POUNDS.
YES, YES, I WILL DO THIS FOR YOU, IF ONLY YOU WILL PLEASE FORGIVE ME AND NOT BE BITTER TOWARD ME...
OH, MISS HAVISHAM, I NEED FORGIVENESS AND DIRECTION FAR TOO MUCH MYSELF TO BE BITTER TOWARD YOU.
OH, WHAT HAVE I DONE...?! WHAT HAVE I DONE...?!
UNTIL YOU SPOKE THE OTHER DAY, AND I SAW IN YOU THE LOOKING-GLASS THAT SHOWED ME WHAT I ONCE FELT MYSELF, I DID NOT REALIZE WHAT I HAD DONE...
YOU'VE DONE NOTHING. I SHOULD HAVE LOVED ESTELLA UNDER ANY CIRCUMSTANCES.
BELIEVE THIS: WHEN SHE CAME TO ME, I ONLY MEANT TO SAVE HER FROM MISERY LIKE MY OWN.
TELL ME... WHOSE CHILD IS ESTELLA?
I DO NOT KNOW. MR. JAGGERS BROUGHT HER TO ME WHEN SHE WAS ONLY THREE — AN ORPHAN.
THEN I LEFT HER ALONE WITH HER MISERABLE THOUGHTS.
WHAT HAVE I DONE...?! WHAT HAVE I DONE...?!

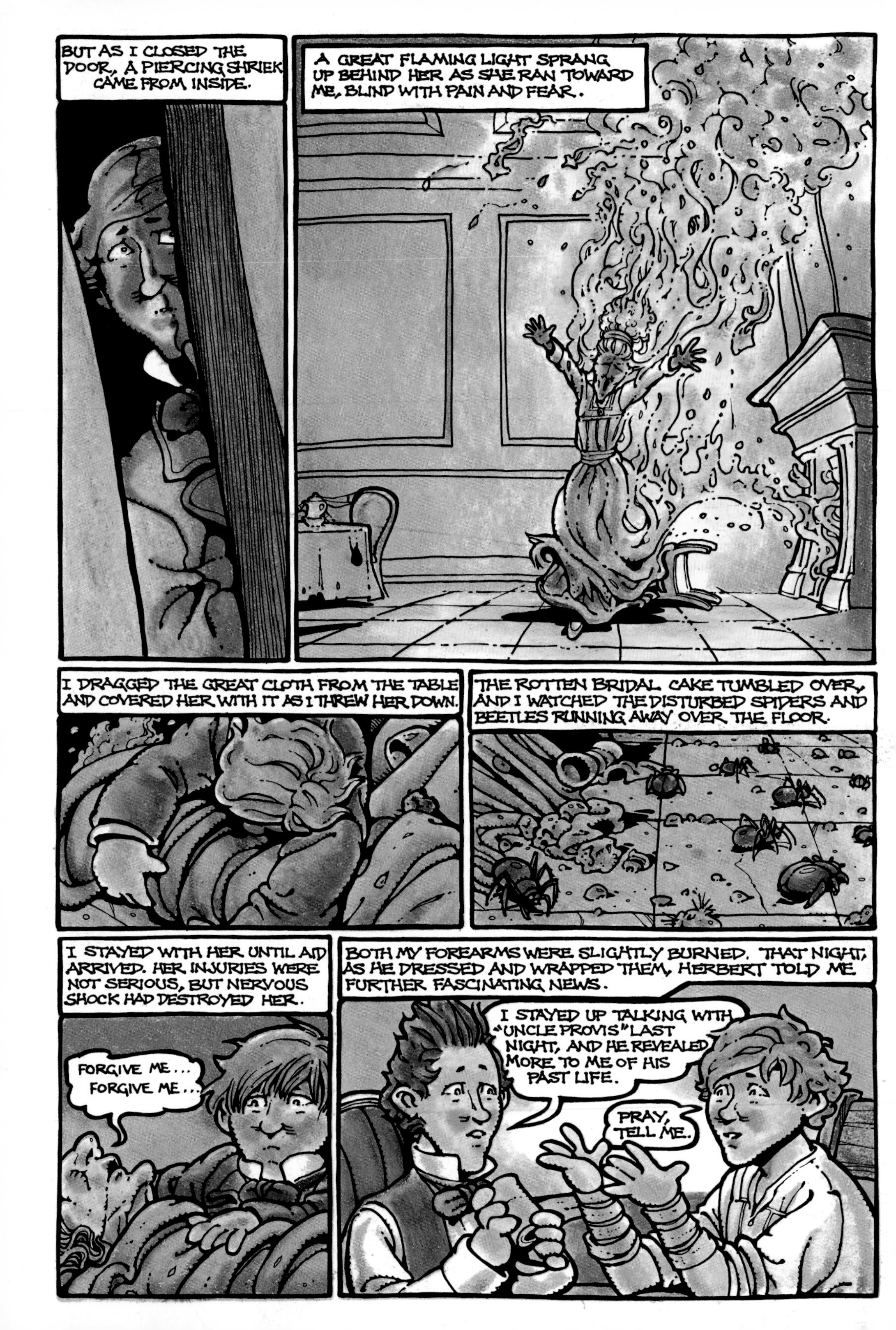

BUT AS I CLOSED THE DOOR, A PIERCING SHRIEK CAME FROM INSIDE.
A GREAT FLAMING LIGHT SPRANG UP BEHIND HER AS SHE RAN TOWARD ME, BLIND WITH PAIN AND FEAR.
I DRAGGED THE GREAT CLOTH FROM THE TABLE AND COVERED HER WITH IT AS I THREW HER DOWN.
THE ROTTEN BRIDAL CAKE TUMBLED OVER, AND I WATCHED THE DISTURBED SPIDERS AND BEETLES RUNNING AWAY OVER THE FLOOR.
I STAYED WITH HER UNTIL AID ARRIVED. HER INJURIES WERE NOT SERIOUS, BUT NERVOUS SHOCK HAD DESTROYED HER.
FORGIVE ME... FORGIVE ME...
BOTH MY FOREARMS WERE SLIGHTLY BURNED. THAT NIGHT, AS HE DRESSED AND WRAPPED THEM, HERBERT TOLD ME FURTHER FASCINATING NEWS.
I STAYED UP TALKING WITH "UNCLE PROVIS" LAST NIGHT, AND HE REVEALED MORE TO ME OF HIS PAST LIFE.
PRAY, TELL ME.

IT SEEMS SOME TWENTY-ODD YEARS AGO, BEFORE HE AND COMPEYSON WERE CAPTURED, HE WAS BREAKING OFF WITH A WOMAN — A HOT-TEMPERED WOMAN HE WAS GREATLY TROUBLED WITH. IT ENDED UP SHE WAS TRIED FOR MURDERING A RIVAL FOR HIS ATTENTION — BUT SHE WAS ACQUITTED.

MOST INTERESTING IS THAT THIS WOMAN AND PROVIS HAD A CHILD — A LITTLE GIRL OF WHOM PROVIS WAS EXCEEDINGLY FOND. HE HAS NO IDEA WHAT HAPPENED TO THE CHILD; HE BELIEVES SHE WAS MURDERED IN A RAGE BY HER MOTHER.

HERBERT, I KNOW THIS IS HARD TO BELIEVE, BUT NOW I AM QUITE CERTAIN THAT THE MAN WE HAVE IN HIDING IS ESTELLA'S FATHER!

AT ONCE, I VISITED MR. JAGGERS TO CONFRONT HIM WITH MY KNOWLEDGE.

SIR, I BELIEVE I KNOW THE IDENTITY OF ESTELLA'S MOTHER. I HAVE SEEN HER THIS WEEK AT YOUR OWN HOUSE. CAN YOU CONFIRM THIS?

I ACKNOWLEDGE NOTHING, MR. PIP... BUT SUCH COULD BE THE CASE.

AND PERHAPS I KNOW MORE OF ESTELLA'S HISTORY THAN YOU DO... I KNOW HER FATHER, TOO. HE IS MAGWITCH, KNOWN AS PROVIS, OF NEW SOUTH WALES.

MR. JAGGERS WAS SPEECHLESS. FOR ONCE, I WAS ABLE TO ASTONISH HIM WITH A PIECE OF INFORMATION.

A FEW DAYS LATER, I RECEIVED A LETTER FROM MR. WEMMICK BY POST.

Early in the week, say Wednesday, you might act upon what we talked of.
Now Burn
W.

AND SO OUR PLAN WENT INTO ACTION. ON WEDNESDAY MORNING, HERBERT AND I PUT PROVIS INTO A BOAT. AIDED BY OUR OLD FRIEND STARTOP, WE ROWED DOWN RIVER WITH THE TIDE.

BY LATE AFTERNOON, WE REACHED A RESTING PLACE BELOW GRAVESEND, WHERE THE RIVER IS BROAD AND SOLITARY. THERE WE SPENT THE NIGHT, NERVOUS AND EXPECTANT OF WHAT WAS TO COME.

IN THE MORNING, WE ROWED TO THE RIVER'S MIDDLE, INTENDING TO HAIL THE STEAMER BOUND FOR HAMBURG, OR THE ONE FOR ROTTERDAM...

PIP, LOOK!

IT WAS A POLICE GALLEY, CLOSING IN QUICKLY TO CUT US OFF. ON BOARD WAS A PRISONER WITH HIS HEAD COVERED.
HO THERE! YOU HAVE A RETURNED TRANSPORT—HIS NAME IS MAGWITCH, OTHERWISE PROVIS! I CALL ON HIM TO SURRENDER!

OUR BOAT WAS SEIZED AND BOARDED — BUT PROVIS LEAPT UP . . .
AND IN A GREAT FURY, HE DIVED UPON THE PRISONER IN THE OTHER BOAT.
IN THE MOMENT BEFORE THEY BOTH DISAPPEARED UNDERWATER, I RECOGNIZED THE OTHER CONVICT OF SO LONG AGO — COMPEYSON!

THE TWO MEN REMAINED UNDER AS THE GREAT STEAMER DISAPPEARED DOWN RIVER, OUR LAST CHANCE GONE.

AT LAST, PROVIS CAME TO THE SURFACE AND WAS BROUGHT ABOARD. HE HAD DISPATCHED THE OTHER, BUT HAD HIMSELF BEEN DEEPLY WOUNDED BY THE SHIP'S PADDLE.

NOW, MY REPUGNANCE OF HIM HAD ALL MELTED AWAY, AND IN THIS POOR CREATURE I SAW ONLY A MAN WHO HAD ACTED AFFECTIONATELY AND GENEROUSLY TOWARDS ME OVER THE YEARS.

I ONLY SAW IN HIM A BETTER MAN THAN I HAD BEEN TO JOE.

I STOOD BESIDE HIM AS HE WAS BROUGHT UP AND SENTENCED. HE KNEW, THOUGH, THAT HIS WOUND WAS MORTAL.
MY LORD, I HAVE RECEIVED MY DEATH SENTENCE FROM THE ALMIGHTY, BUT I BOW TO YOURS.
I FELT THAT MY PLACE WAS AT HIS SIDE HENCEFORTH WHILE HE LIVED.
I AM GRIEVED TO THINK YOU CAME BACK FOR MY SAKE.
DEAR PIP, I WAS QUITE CONTENT TO TAKE MY CHANCE. NOW I'VE SEEN MY LAD, AND HE CAN BE A GENTLEMAN WITHOUT ME.
GOD BLESS YOU, DEAR BOY — YOU'VE NEVER DESERTED ME.
AS HE BREATHED HIS LAST, I TOLD HIM WHAT I KNEW.
YOU HAD A CHILD ONCE WHOM YOU LOVED AND LOST . . . SHE LIVED AND FOUND POWERFUL FRIENDS. SHE IS LIVING NOW: SHE IS A LADY AND VERY BEAUTIFUL . . . AND I LOVE HER!
IN THAT SAME WEEK, I SAID FAREWELL TO HERBERT. HE WAS EAGER AND HOPEFUL ABOUT HIS NEW POSITION AS HEAD OF CLARRIKER'S OFFICE IN FAR-OFF ALEXANDRIA.
WHEN I'M SETTLED, I WILL SEND FOR CLARA. I SHALL NEVER FORGET YOU, DEAR FRIEND.
NOR I YOU. WE WILL WRITE EACH OTHER OFTEN, DON'T FORGET!
NOW I WAS TRULY ADRIFT. I HAD NO MORE INCOME: ALL OF MAGWITCH'S PROPERTY WAS TAKEN BY THE CROWN. I HAD NO HOME AND NO FRIENDS AND NO PROSPECTS.
ALL I COULD DO WAS FALL INTO A DEEP FEVER. I LAY INSENSIBLE FOR A TIME THAT SEEMED INTERMINABLE — ALL THE WHILE PLAGUED BY FEARFUL DREAMS. BUT AS I REACHED THE LOWEST POINT OF MY ILLNESS, THE GENTLE FACE OF JOE KEPT FLOATING INTO VIEW.

AT LAST, THE FOG LIFTED, AND I SLOWLY OPENED MY EYES.
IT IS JOE!
WHICH IT ARE, OLD CHAP.

DEAR JOE — IS IT REALLY YOU?
YES, PIP, WHICH YOU AND ME WAS EVER THE BEST OF FRIENDS.

JOE CARED FOR ME TENDERLY THROUGH THE LONG WEEKS OF MY RECOVERY. HE EVEN USED HIS SAVINGS TO PAY OFF MY LINGERING DEBTS.

BUT, AS I BECAME MORE MYSELF, HE BEGAN TO SLOWLY WITHDRAW FROM ME.

YOU'VE ALMOST COME 'ROUND NOW, PIP. IT LOOKS LIKE TIME FOR ME TO GO BACK TO THE FORGE.

DESPITE MY ENTREATIES, HE DETACHED HIMSELF FROM ME AND LEFT FOR HOME.

WHAT COULD I DO BUT FOLLOW?

I HOPED TO LET JOE AND BIDDY SEE HOW HUMBLED AND REPENTENT I WAS — PERHAPS THEN I COULD ONCE AGAIN ENTER THEIR LIVES.

BIDDY RUSHED TO EMBRACE ME WHEN I WALKED IN. WE WEPT TO SEE EACH OTHER.
OUR PIP IS HOME!

WHAT MORE COULD I WANT? IT'S MY WEDDING DAY, PIP, AND I AM MARRIED TO JOE!

DEAR BIDDY, YOU HAVE THE BEST HUSBAND IN THE WORLD! I WISH YOU BOTH JOY, AND I WISH FOR MYSELF TO BE A LITTLE WORTHIER OF YOU THAN I WAS — NOT MUCH, BUT A LITTLE.

IT WAS ELEVEN YEARS BEFORE I AGAIN VISITED MY VILLAGE ON THE MARSHES. DURING THAT TIME I HAD LIVED QUIETLY IN ALEXANDRIA WITH HERBERT AND CLARA, AND HAD WORKED MY WAY TO A POSITION OF RESPONSIBILITY WITH CLARRIKER & CO.

UPON MY RETURN, I STOPPED AT THE LONELY RUINS OF SATIS HOUSE.
ESTELLA!
WHY, PIP! I AM GREATLY CHANGED. I WONDER YOU KNOW ME.

I HAD HEARD OF HER LEADING A MOST UNHAPPY LIFE. HER HUSBAND HAD USED HER CRUELLY, AND AFTER HIS DEATH—CONSEQUENT TO THE ILL-TREATMENT OF A HORSE—SHE HAD LIVED ABROAD.

I HAVE OFTEN THOUGHT OF YOU.

AND YOU MUST KNOW YOU HAVE ALWAYS HELD A PLACE IN MY HEART.

YOU ONCE SAID TO ME, "GOD FORGIVE YOU." IF YOU COULD SAY IT THEN, PLEASE BE AS GOOD TO ME NOW, AND TELL ME WE ARE FRIENDS.

YES, ESTELLA, WE ARE FRIENDS.
AND WILL CONTINUE FRIENDS APART.

IT WAS THEN I HAD THE ASSURANCE THAT HER SUFFERING HAD BEEN STRONGER THAN MISS HAVISHAM'S TEACHING, AND HAD GIVEN HER A HEART TO UNDERSTAND WHAT MY HEART USED TO BE.

AND I TOOK HER HAND IN MINE, AND WE LEFT THAT RUINED PLACE. THE EVENING MISTS WERE RISING, AND IN ALL THE BROAD EXPANSE OF TRANQUIL LIGHT THEY SHOWED ME, I SAW NO SHADOW OF ANOTHER PARTING FROM HER.
THE END.

WATCH OUT FOR PAPERCUTZ™

Welcome to the premiere Papercutz edition of CLASSICS ILLUSTRATED. I'm Jim Salicrup, Papercutz Editor-in-Chief, and proud to be associated with such a legendary comicbook series. If you're unfamiliar with Papercutz, let me quickly say that we're the graphic novel publishers of such titles as BIONICLE, NANCY DREW, THE HARDY BOYS, TALES FROM THE CRYPT, and now, CLASSICS ILLUSTRATED and CLASSICS ILLUSTRATED DELUXE. In the backpages of our titles, we usually run a section, aptly named "the Papercutz Backpages," which is devoted to letting you know all that's happening at Papercutz. You can also check us out at www.papercutz.com for even more information and previews of upcoming Papercuts graphic novels. But this time around, the big news is CLASSICS ILLUSTRATED!

You see, even though I've been in the world of comics for thirty-five years, I'm still very much the same comicbook fan I was when I was a kid! And if my partner, Papercutz Publisher, Terry Nantier, were to magically go back in time, and tell 13 year-old Jim Salicrup that he was going to one day be the editor of NANCY DREW, THE HARDY BOYS, TALES FROM THE CRYPT, and CLASSICS ILLUSTRATED, he'd think Terry was out of his mind!

Let's get real. Back then I'd see CLASSICS ILLUSTRATED comics in their own display rack, apart from all the other comicbooks, at my favorite soda shoppe in the Bronx. Each issue featured a comics adaptation of a classic novel-that's why they called it CLASSICS ILLUSTRATED. But unlike other comicbooks, these were bigger, containing 48 pages per book; cost a quarter, more than twice as much as a regular 12 cent comic; and stayed on sale forever, as opposed to the other comics which were gone in a month. Clearly, these comics were something special.

Bah, I can take a gazillion moments, but this is still way too humungous an event for my puny brain to fully absorb, so I'm going to give up trying and accept that we here at Papercutz must be doing something right to be entrusted with Comicdom's crown jewels! So no more looking back--time to focus on the future. That means doing everything we can to make sure these titles live up to their proud heritage, while gaining a whole new generation of fans.

On the following pages, enjoy Marion Mousse's amazing adaptation of Mary Shelley's FRANKENSTEIN – a special preview of CLASSICS ILLUSTRATED DELUXE #3.

As usual, you can contact me at salicrup@papercutz.com or Jim Salicrup, PAPERCUTZ, 40 Exchange Place, Ste. 1308, New York, NY 10005 and let us know how we're doing. After all, we want you to be as excited about Papercutz as we are!

Thanks,

Caricature drawn by Steve Brodner at the MoCCA Art Fest.

FOR MORE THAN A YEAR, I STUDIED ALL THE FORMS AND CONSE-QUENCES OF DEATH: THE FLESH DECOMPOSING, SLOWLY ROTTING...

...THE MATTER OF WHICH WE'RE ALL MADE, DEGRADING AND WASTING AWAY BEFORE VANISHING AS THOUGH THROUGH MAGIC.

FRANKENSTEIN...
...OUR LOCAL CELEBRITY HARD AT WORK.
...

DOCTOR KREMPE...
YOUR WHIMSICAL THEORIES ARE THE MOCKERY OF ALL INGOLSTADT, FRANKEN-STEIN!
WHY THEN? IF YOU PREFER DIGGING THROUGH FLESH TO DELIGHTING IN THAT CREDULOUS AUDIENCE.

STILL CHASING AFTER YOUR MAD HEROES?! CORNELIUS AGRIPPA, PARACELSUS...
DON'T TELL ME THAT YOU'RE STILL A DISCIPLE OF THOSE COOKED-UP ABSURDITIES?!

PHILLIPUS AUREOLUS VON HOHENHEIM, KNOWN AS PARACELSUS, EMINENT ALCHEMIST, WHO CLAIMED TO HAVE EXPERIMENTED ON THE FAMOUS ELIXIR OF ETERNAL YOUTH AND CREATED...

...THE HOMUNCU-LUS, A SMALL LIVING BEING IN THE FORM OF A HUMAN!
I KNOW ALL THAT, FRANKENSTEIN!
SO YOU CONTINUE AND CONTINUE TO PERSIST! YOU PERSIST IN RIDICULING YOUR PROFESSORS, IN DISCREDITING OUR HON-ORABLE INSTITUTION?!!

WELL THEN! SO, I HEREAFTER FORBID YOU TO USE COURSE MATERIAL SUCH AS HUMAN REMAINS OUTSIDE OF YOUR COURSES!
UNTIL NOW, I'D MADE NO ASSUMPTIONS ABOUT YOUR CHARACTER, YOUNG MAN.

YES, I WAS HESITATING...I WAS HESITATING BETWEEN A YAHOO AND AN ENLIGHTENED SCIENTIST...NOW I KNOW.

A YAHOO!!
DO YOU HEAR, THEODORE?!

THAT OLD, PRETENTIOUS, BACKWARDS IMBECILE TREATED ME...
STOP...

VICTOR, STOP, I BEG YOU.

THEO...
YOU CAN'T, YOU HEAR, VICTOR? YOU CAN'T!
CHOOSING TO DISSECT A CORPSE, AGAINST THE SACROSANCT PRINCIPLE OF UNITY THAT UNDERLIES THE NOTION OF THE INDIVIDUAL, IS ALREADY A BLASPHEMY ACCORDING TO THE COMMITTEE!

BUT CLAIMING TO RECREATE THAT UNITY AND GIVING LIFE BACK TO IT...
... IT'S PURE FOLLY!!

THERE'S AN ESSENTIAL FACT, MY GOOD THEO, TRANSCENDING THE TRANSCENDENTAL!
AH! VICTOR...

THEO...
THEO, WHAT YOU'RE TALKING ABOUT IS RIDICULOUS! YOU'RE NOT EVEN A BELIEVER!
I DON'T RECOGNIZE YOU.

ME EITHER, VICTOR, ME EITHER.

ANYWAYS, DON'T WORRY, THE LABORATORIES ARE NOW CLOSED TO ME, I NO LONGER HAVE...
....ANY VICTIMS UPON WHOM TO PERPETRATE MY CRIMES! SO BE GLAD!!

I'VE LEFT SEVERAL BOOKS FOR YOU ON THE COUNTER... FROM DOCTOR WALDMAN.

THIS WAY, YOUNG MAN.

...
THE KEY...

AH, THE KEY TO PARADISE! CHOLERA, TYPHUS, COAL, ETC, A GIFT FROM HEAVEN FOR VAMPIRES.

SLOWLY, I CUT MYSELF OFF FROM EVERYONE AND INVITED MYSELF INTO THAT OTHER WORLD I WOULD NO LONGER LEAVE BEHIND.

HE SEEMS RATHER YOUNG TO BE UNDERTAKING THIS SORT OF THING.

THAT'S WHERE HE'LL SUCCEED OR FAIL. HE MUST TRY. OTHERWISE, HE'LL END UP BEING CONSUMED BY FEAR AND REGRET.
IT'S NOW OR NEVER.

HE'S GIFTED, MARKUS...MAYBE TOO MUCH SO.

WINTER, SPRING, AND SUMMER PASSED AWAY DURING MY LABORS; BUT I DID NOT WATCH THE BLOSSOM OR THE EXPANDING LEAVES--SIGHTS WHICH BEFORE ALWAYS YIELDED ME SUPREME DELIGHT.

I WAS EXHAUSTING MYSELF OVER ROTTING FLESH. MY NIGHTMARES TEMPERING MY ENTHUSIASM, ONLY THE ENERGY RESULTING FROM MY RESOLVE SUSTAINED ME.

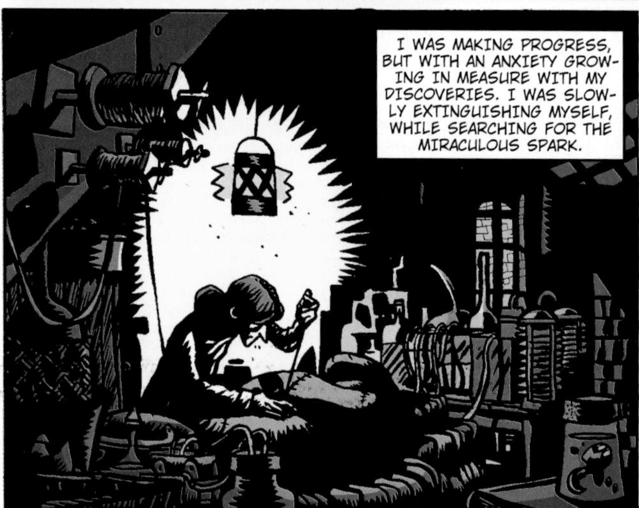
I WAS MAKING PROGRESS, BUT WITH AN ANXIETY GROWING IN MEASURE WITH MY DISCOVERIES. I WAS SLOWLY EXTINGUISHING MYSELF, WHILE SEARCHING FOR THE MIRACULOUS SPARK.

RELENTLESSLY ON THE HUNT FOR THIS SPARK, I SCANNED THE HEAVENS AND BEGGED THEM TO BURST FORTH IN STORM. HOW IRONIC, NO? I WAS HOPING FOR RESURRECTION FROM THE SKY.

"WE'RE BACK!"
JACK LAKE
PRODUCTIONS INC.
CLASSICS Illustrated
THE THREE MUSKETEERS
Alexandre Dumas
THE LAST OF THE MOHICANS
MOBY DICK
Herman Melville
GULLIVER'S TRAVELS
HUCKLEBERRY FINN
FRANKENSTEIN
MARY W. SHELLEY
SWISS FAMILY ROBINSON
Johann Wyss
20,000 LEAGUES UNDER THE SEA
BLACK BEAUTY
TREASURE ISLAND
THE CALL OF THE WILD
THE TIME MACHINE
H. G. WELLS
ROMEO and JULIET
William Shakespeare
THE AENEID
A JOURNEY TO THE CENTER OF THE EARTH
JULES VERNE
The Story of AMERICA
THE WAR BETWEEN THE STATES
Special Issue
FREE
36" x 27"
POSTER
with purchase of 10 or more titles.

RICK GEARY

Rick Geary was born in 1946 in Kansas City, Missouri and grew up in Wichita, Kansas. He graduated from the University of Kansas in Lawrence, where his first cartoons were published in the University Daily Kansan.

He worked as staff artist for two weekly papers in Wichita before moving to San Diego in 1975.

He began work in comics in 1977 and was for thirteen years a contributor to the Funny Pages of National Lampoon. His comic stories have also been published in Heavy Metal, Dark Horse Comics and the DC Comics/Paradox Press Big Books. His early comic work has been collected in Housebound with Rick Geary from Fantagraphics Books.

During a four-year stay in New York, his illustrations appeared regularly in The New York Times Book Review. His illustration work has also been seen in MAD, Spy, Rolling Stone, The Los Angeles Times, and American Libraries.

He has written and illustrated three children's books based on The Mask for Dark Horse and two Spider-Man children's books for Marvel. His children's comic Society of Horrors ran in Disney Adventures magazine from 1999 to 2006. He is currently the artist for the new series of Gumby comics, written by Bob Burden.

His graphic novels include three adaptations for CLASSICS ILLUSTRATED and the continuing series A Treasury of Victorian Murder for NBM Publishing, the latest of which is The Lindbergh Child. In 2007, he wrote and illustrated J. Edgar Hoover: A Graphic Biography for Farrar, Straus and Giroux.

Rick has received the Inkpot Award from the San Diego Comic Convention (1980), the Book and Magazine Illustration Award from the National Cartoonists Society (1994), and the Eisner Award (2007).

He and his wife Deborah can be found every year in the Artists Alley at San Diego Comic Con International. In 2007, after more than thirty years in San Diego, they moved to the town of Carrizozo, New Mexico.